I0713353

Winter at Saddle Creek

A Fast-Paced Horse Barn Storm Adventure for Young Riders and Horse Lovers

The Saddle Creek Riders

Book 4

Wren Jane Willowbrook

Contents

Chapter One

The first snow of the year always arrived quietly at Saddle Creek, as if winter preferred to tiptoe across the valley rather than announce itself. It came in the night, settling over the rooftops and fences and pasture hills in a soft white blanket. When Emma stepped out of her mother's car that morning, she breathed the cold air slowly, letting it sink into her chest like a promise that something new was beginning.

Everything felt calmer than it had in weeks. The fall season had been full of noise and tension. The medal final had pushed everyone harder than they expected. Knightfall had refused that one jump that looked harmless to everyone except him. Emma had replayed it in her mind again and again. She remembered the way his ears flattened and how his stride faltered. She remembered the shock in her stomach when it happened. She remembered how Riley was convinced that he sensed something odd on the ground and how Zoey had tried to back up that idea with half-baked theories she found online. In the end it did not matter. The season had ended, and Knightfall was still her horse. Her partner. Her friend.

Winter felt like a clean page. Maybe even a healing one.

She kicked through the crunchy snow on the walkway and pulled her jacket tighter around her. The barn doors stood half open, letting warm air drift out in a faint mist. She loved that sight so much she paused for a full breath before stepping inside.

Inside, Saddle Creek smelled like hay, cinnamon from Coach's morning tea, and horses settling into winter routines. The aisle was swept neatly, though a few flakes were melting where someone had tracked them in. A row of horses peeked out from their stalls, ears forward, noses already searching pockets for treats.

Emma smiled. Knightfall's coppery ears stuck over the stall door even before she reached him. He recognized the sound of her footsteps without fail.

"Morning, handsome," she said softly.

He nickered and pressed his forehead to her shoulder. His coat felt extra warm against her chilled fingers. She rubbed his cheek and checked the tightness of his blanket straps. Everything looked right. He pawed once, impatient for breakfast or attention or maybe both.

"You look too clean. Did you roll already?" she teased.

Knightfall lifted his head proudly, which was as much of a confession as she was going to get.

Down the aisle, Zoey appeared with a bucket of warm mash balanced in both hands. Her curly hair was tucked into a knitted beanie the exact color of snowberries. Her eyes found Emma immediately.

"Beautiful out there this morning," Zoey said as she hooked the bucket over a stall bar. "Almost like the valley got dunked in powdered sugar."

"Except the part we have to shovel later," Emma replied.

Zoey grinned. "Details. My aunt says this snow means we are in for a real winter this year. She also said my cousin might be visiting this summer. The one who works with backcountry horses in Montana. She is like a wilderness whisperer or whatever my aunt calls her."

"That sounds incredible," Emma said. "Do you think she will bring a horse?"

"I hope so. She travels with two sometimes. They can handle cliffs and rivers like it is nothing. She rides for hours without worrying about anything other than weather and wild life. Honestly it makes our trail rides look like gentle strolls." Zoey's face lit up with excitement. "If she comes, I am asking her to teach me everything."

Emma opened Knightfall's stall and stepped inside. Zoey followed and leaned on the doorframe. The horse lowered his head so Emma could check under his blanket. Everything looked healthy and relaxed.

After a moment Zoey's voice softened. "Does it feel strange yet?"

"Strange?" Emma asked.

"You know. Being back at the barn after the medal final. It was intense for everyone."

Emma took a slow breath. "It feels better, actually. Like nothing is chasing us anymore."

"I feel that too." Zoey nudged the straw with her boot. "Even Riley seemed calmer today. She did not snap at anyone during feed time."

Emma chuckled. "Give it an hour."

They both knew Riley loved the barn more than anything in the world, but winter tested her patience. She hated when the indoor felt crowded and when Ruby's energy doubled because the pastures were too snowy for turnout. Riley would never admit it, but cold weather made her more emotional. She felt every frustration like it was personal.

Before Emma could answer, the barn door swung open again. Riley marched in wearing a coat that looked too thin for the temperature, her plait swinging behind her like a determined flag. She brushed snow off her shoulders and muttered something no one could hear.

"Speak of the storm," Zoey whispered.

Riley stopped short when she saw them both. "What are you two staring at?"

"Nothing," Zoey said cheerfully. "Just enjoying the beauty of winter and the miracle that you are awake before nine."

Riley rolled her eyes, though a small smile tugged at her mouth. "I woke up freezing because my window got stuck open again. Then I had to dig out my driveway so my mom could take my brother to school. So forgive me if I am not singing holiday songs yet."

Emma stepped out of Knightfall's stall. "We were about to tack up for a light ride. You coming?"

"Indoor?" Riley asked.

"Indoor," Emma confirmed.

Riley groaned. "Ruby is already bouncing off the walls. She is going to act like she has never seen another horse before."

Zoey lifted an eyebrow. "And whose job is it to help her with that?"

Riley crossed her arms. "Do not start."

Emma sensed the tension inching upward. She nudged Zoey gently and changed the subject.

"Coach said something earlier," she said. "I am not sure what it means but she mentioned a rumor about a spring clinic. Something big."

Riley paused. "Like hosted here?"

"I think so," Emma answered.

Zoey's face illuminated. "Imagine if they bring someone famous."

"I hope it is someone who understands nervous horses," Emma said. She glanced at Knightfall. "He could use fresh eyes."

"Or someone who can help with rider confidence," Zoey added. "After last season I would not mind a boost."

Riley put her hands on her hips. "It will not matter who they bring if our indoor turns into a madhouse all winter. We need actual practice space."

Emma nodded. "Coach knows we need help. She has been talking about new funding too."

"It better come through," Riley muttered. "If one more person cuts me off in the corners I might scream."

Zoey tapped her shoulder. "New year. New patience."

"Not happening," Riley replied.

Emma laughed under her breath. It felt good to hear the familiar bickering again. As much as their dynamic changed during the fall, beneath the competition stress there was still loyalty and friendship. Winter had a way of pulling them closer again.

They walked together toward the tack room. The old wooden sign above the door read Saddle Creek Riders and carried faint chips where past students had bumped it with saddles. Inside, everything felt warm and slightly cramped, packed with bridles, saddle pads, grooming kits, and a row of hooks overflowing with winter gloves.

Knightfall's bridle hung from the third hook on the left. Emma traced the leather before lifting it carefully. She liked to check each buckle in winter since cold weather stiffened the straps.

Zoey grabbed her saddle pad and hummed a tune that made Emma laugh. "What are you singing?"

"Something my cousin taught me. She says humming calms nervous horses during storms." Zoey paused dramatically. "Which might be helpful tonight."

Riley groaned from across the room. "Please do not jinx us. We have had enough storms for one lifetime."

Emma felt the tension ripple just a little. For a brief second she remembered the chaotic moments from the medal final when rumors had spread and alliances shifted. That had been hard on everyone, especially Riley and Zoey. She hoped the new season would mend whatever cracks remained.

With tack in hand they headed back to the aisle. Snow dazzled outside the windows, swirling in lazy circles as it fell. Emma felt the cold seep through the cracks in the big barn doors. She fastened Knightfall's halter, led him into the cross ties, and began brushing him.

He was extra fuzzy today. His winter coat had grown thick

enough to trap warmth. As she brushed, he stretched his neck out and sighed. That was his way of saying he trusted her completely, and it melted her every time.

Zoey passed behind them with a curry comb. "He looks too perfect. Ruby is going to look like a wind-blown mop next to him."

"Ruby always looks dramatic," Riley said. She clipped a cooler over Ruby's back and tried to smooth her own hair at the same time.

"Drama is a lifestyle for her," Zoey replied. "Like someone else I know."

Riley snapped a towel in her direction, but Zoey dodged it easily.

Emma suppressed a smile and focused on Knightfall. She lifted his hooves, knocked out a few bits of packed snow, then checked his shoes. Everything was in order. She placed the saddle pad across his back and settled the saddle gently on top.

Out in the aisle, the sound of the big barn door creaking open again signaled Coach's arrival. She entered with a steaming mug in her hand, her scarf wrapped high around her chin.

"Morning, girls," Coach said. "First snow means first indoor safety reminders. Respect spacing. Keep your lines clean. No sudden changes of direction. Horses are fresh today so pay attention to each other. The footing was dragged an hour ago, but if the wind keeps pushing cold air in we will have to keep sessions short."

"Yes, Coach," the girls chorused.

Coach nodded with satisfaction. "And keep an ear out at lunch. I might have some news about spring."

Zoey clapped her hands once. Riley locked eyes with Emma, excitement flickering there despite her moody morning. Emma felt her heart lift. Winter felt like a pause from pressure but a beginning of opportunity too.

They finished tacking up and walked their horses toward the arena. The corridor to the indoor had always fascinated Emma. The narrow passage held old ribbons and framed photos from previous Saddle Creek riders. There were pictures of girls who had grown up, moved away, and left their mark in neat wooden frames. There were also photos of horses who had retired long ago. Knightfall was not on that wall yet, though Emma sometimes imagined him there one day.

When they reached the indoor arena, a burst of warm air hit them. The heaters hummed overhead. The arena lights cast a golden glow over the sand. The mirrors at the far end reflected the horses walking in, creating doubled images that shimmered softly in the brightness.

Emma mounted carefully and settled into the saddle. Knightfall shifted under her with a little hop of enthusiasm.

"Easy," Emma said, patting his neck.

Zoey mounted her mare, Daisy, who looked half asleep. Riley swung onto Ruby, who bounced in place the moment she felt the reins shorten.

"Calm down," Riley muttered. "Your brain is frozen or something."

Zoey laughed. "She is excited because she likes winter."

"Or she likes watching me freeze," Riley replied.

They walked their horses around the perimeter, warming up at a slow pace. Knightfall's ears flicked forward and back as he observed everything. The sound of Ruby snorting. The rustle of Zoey's jacket. The creak of leather. The squeak of the arena door closing.

Emma took a deep breath and let it go. This was home. Even with memories of the medal final lingering in the corners of her mind, the indoor felt safe today.

Coach stepped to the center of the ring and clapped once. "Walk to trot transitions. Make it smooth."

Emma lifted her hands slightly and asked Knightfall to trot. He responded instantly, yet with softness, like he was offering a fresh start too. She posted lightly, feeling each stride steady under her.

Riley steered Ruby into a diagonal line. Ruby tossed her head and kicked out playfully. Riley sighed loudly and repeated the transition.

Zoey's mare trotted with long, floating strides. Daisy looked beautiful, even in winter mode. Zoey beamed with pride.

Coach watched each rider in turn. "Emma, he looks more

balanced today. Riley, shorten your reins but relax your fingers. Zoey, keep that outside elbow soft."

As they rode, the snow kept falling beyond the windows, thick flakes drifting down like feathers. The outdoor jumps were nearly hidden under a rising blanket of white. Saddle Creek looked peaceful, almost magical.

It struck Emma that this winter would be different from the last. She was stronger now. Knightfall was more confident. Their team, though a little bruised from fall drama, felt whole again or at least on the way to healing.

After a while Coach signaled for a walk break. The horses stretched their necks and blew warm breath into the chilly air.

"That felt better," Zoey said as she joined Emma near the rail.

"Knightfall felt so steady," Emma replied. "Like the snow quieted his mind."

"Maybe it did." Zoey leaned on her pommel. "Winter is like a reset button."

Emma smiled. "A reset sounds good."

Riley guided Ruby around to them. "She is losing her mind today, but we will work through it. If I can survive winter rides with her, I can survive anything."

Zoey snorted. "I doubt that."

Riley narrowed her eyes. "What does that mean?"

"It means you get dramatic when you are cold," Zoey teased.

"Me?" Riley sputtered. "You are the one who wears five scarves and complains that your eyelashes are freezing."

"Only once," Zoey insisted. "And it was actually freezing rain."

Emma giggled. "You two sound like sisters."

Zoey grinned. Riley pretended not to smile.

Coach called for canter transitions next. Emma guided Knightfall forward. He lifted into canter with a calmness that surprised her. For the next several minutes she worked through circles, serpentines, and careful bends. She remembered every lesson from fall, every correction, every success. It all added up now.

When they switched reins, Emma caught a glimpse of the viewing loft above the arena. A group of younger riders watched, their cheeks pink from the cold. They whispered excitedly, probably imagining themselves cantering like that one day. Emma used to stand up there and imagine the same thing. Now she was here, in the saddle, growing every season.

After the last canter work, Coach called for cool down. The horses slowed to a walk with soft snorts.

"Good work," Coach said. "That is a solid start to winter training. Now get your horses warm, get them fed, and get yourselves some hot chocolate. You all earned it."

Riley pumped a fist. "Best words I have heard all morning."

They unmounted and walked their horses out of the ring. Snow still drifted past the arena windows, thicker now, swirling in slow loops that looked almost playful. Emma led Knightfall to the barn, his hooves crunching through scattered bits of snow by the doorway.

Back in the aisle, she removed his tack and replaced it with a cozy fleece cooler. Knightfall flicked his ears and nudged her gently, almost as if thanking her.

"You did great today," Emma whispered, smoothing the cooler along his back. "Today felt right."

Zoey passed behind her. "You know, if that spring clinic rumor is real, we should start planning early. We could put together a wishlist of what we want to learn."

Riley snorted. "My list is simple. I want Ruby to stop acting like the world is ending every time it snows."

Zoey laughed. "That is not going to happen."

"She can change," Riley insisted.

"Maybe with your cousin's wilderness training," Emma added.

Zoey brightened. "Exactly. If she visits this summer, we could try trail challenges or long rides or maybe even overnight camping. She knows everything about mountain horses. Real adventure stuff."

Riley stuck her tongue out at her. "You love making us suffer."

"You love pretending you hate it," Zoey said.

Emma smiled at both of them. Their arguing today felt softer, almost affectionate. Winter softened edges that fall had sharpened too much.

She led Knightfall back into his stall. He turned immediately to his hay net and took a long contented chew. Emma stroked his neck before stepping out.

The barn lights glowed warmly behind her as she walked down the aisle. Snowflakes drifted through the open door like glitter being poured from the sky.

She paused to look out at the pasture. Snow blanketed the ground and softened all the fences and shadows. The world felt clean. Quiet. Ready.

Winter at Saddle Creek had begun. And with it came new chances, new challenges, and new stories waiting to unfold.

Emma felt it in the air. Something good was coming. Something that stretched beyond the cold months and into spring. She could not name it yet, but she could feel its shape, like a hint of light behind a cloud.

She took one last breath of cold morning air and stepped fully into the barn again, warmed by the knowledge that whatever came next, she and Knightfall would face it together.

Chapter Two

The snow had thickened through the afternoon, falling in slow, steady drifts that made Saddle Creek look almost dreamlike. By the time Emma returned after lunch, the parking lot held deep footprints, and the arena roof hummed under the steady tap of sleet. The morning had felt peaceful, almost magical, but winter had its own way of shifting moods as the day stretched on. Coach always said that winter riding demanded patience. Emma understood that in theory. Living it was something else.

Her boots crunched as she crossed the yard again. Snowflakes melted against her cheeks. She inhaled deeply, loving the bite of cold air even though it tightened her lungs for a moment. The barn doors were closed now, holding in warmth like a giant thermos. She knocked off snow from her gloves and tugged the handle open.

Inside, the air felt thicker and busier than it had earlier. Horses blew warm breaths into the aisle. A group lesson of younger riders had just finished, and the kids were rushing to untack their ponies with the clumsy excitement that only winter could bring. Two ponies sneezed at the same time, showering sawdust over the straw. One of the girls squealed in delight. Coach raised an eyebrow but did not comment.

Emma scanned the hallway for Knightfall's stall. He poked his head out the moment he saw her, ears high, eyes bright. She walked to him immediately, reaching to scratch under his jaw.

"Miss me already?" she whispered.

Knightfall exhaled a warm breath right on her face. She laughed, brushing snow from her hair.

Harper walked past carrying an armful of saddle pads. Her cheeks glowed pink from the cold, and her blond braid was dusted with snowflakes. She paused when she saw Emma.

"You here for the afternoon ride?" Harper asked, shifting the pads to her other arm.

"That is the plan," Emma said. "It looks crowded."

Harper laughed softly. "Crowded is an understatement. The indoor looks like rush hour in a city tunnel. Coach said the snow might get worse tonight, so she is trying to squeeze in as many lessons as possible before the wind picks up."

Emma glanced toward the indoor arena entrance. The muffled sound of hooves echoed from inside, along with the occasional voice of Coach correcting someone's posture.

"Is Zoey here yet?" Emma asked.

"Just arrived," Harper replied. "She is changing Daisy's saddle pad right now. And Riley is in one of her moods again."

Emma felt a faint tightening in her stomach. "How bad?"

Harper gave a half grimace. "Not catastrophic. Just... Riley-ish."

Emma smirked. "Got it."

Harper nodded sympathetically and moved on toward the tack room, her arms full of soft fabric.

Emma focused on Knightfall. She slipped into his stall and loosened the top of his blanket. His winter coat shone beneath the soft fleece lining. He flicked his tail once, then nudged her jacket.

"I know," she said gently. "You want to work again."

He bobbed his head, as if agreeing.

She took a few quiet minutes brushing him inside the stall. His coat had fluffed up a bit more since the morning, which made him look like a large, elegant puffball. Emma smiled, running her brush down his shoulder.

As she concentrated on grooming, the barn door creaked open again and Zoey hurried in, carrying a saddle pad with a bright blue trim. Snowflakes clung to her beanie and eyelashes.

"There you are," Zoey said breathlessly. "I thought maybe you got snowed in."

"Not yet," Emma said. "But if it keeps falling like this, we might need sleds to get home."

Zoey laughed and set her saddle pad down. "Daisy's in a weird mood. Not spooky exactly. More like extra alert. I think the cold has her ready to launch into orbit."

"Knightfall is calm," Emma said. "Probably because he worked earlier."

"That helps," Zoey said. "Riley did not ride Ruby this morning though. She said she needed time to reset after her chaotic morning. I did not argue. It was safer that way."

Emma raised a brow. "Is she alright?"

Zoey exhaled slowly, tugging at the edge of her beanie. "I do not know. She is acting prickly, but she has been like that every winter we have known her. Cold weather is like fuel for her temper."

Emma nodded. "Ruby too."

Zoey giggled. "Maybe that is why they get along so well."

Emma stepped out of Knightfall's stall and latched the door. As she carried her grooming kit to the cross ties, she saw Riley leading Ruby from the far end of the barn. Ruby walked with her neck high and steps springy, nostrils flaring at the drifting snow visible through the small window near the ceiling.

Riley looked exactly how Emma expected. Determined jaw. Slightly narrowed eyes. Shoulders squared like someone preparing for a challenge she was already tired of facing. Ruby tossed her head, swinging her mane into Riley's face.

Riley clicked her tongue sharply. "Quit it."

Zoey whispered under her breath to Emma. "Storm incoming."

Emma shot her a quick look. "Be nice."

Zoey raised her hands in surrender.

Riley joined them in the aisle, clipping Ruby into the cross ties with brisk movements.

"You riding now?" Emma asked gently.

"Obviously," Riley replied. Then she sighed. "Sorry. Yes. I am riding now. Ruby is acting like she drank five litres of coffee and inhaled the snow drift outside."

Ruby let out a loud snort as if confirming it.

Zoey smothered a laugh. "She does look thrilled with life."

Riley glared. "Not helping."

Zoey winked. "Just observing."

Emma stepped slightly between them. "Maybe the indoor will help Ruby settle."

Riley gave a doubtful grunt but did not say anything else. She pulled her saddle from its rack and set it on Ruby's back, her fingers working efficiently even though her frustration showed.

The barn aisle bustled with the last of the younger riders finishing their lessons. Parents poked their heads inside occasionally to call out reminders about homework or snacks. A pony sneezed loudly enough to startle a girl into dropping a curry comb. The small chaos of winter afternoons filled every corner.

As the younger group cleared out, Coach stepped into the aisle. She scanned the room, assessing the energy instantly.

"Alright, girls," Coach said. "This session is going to be a tight squeeze. The indoor is full of riders who were supposed to be outdoors today. I need everyone calm, focused, and flexible. We will rotate exercises to avoid crowding. Half arena at a time. No cutting corners, and keep your tempers in check."

Riley muttered something under her breath. Zoey smirked. Emma prayed they would not explode at each other.

Coach lifted a brow. "Did someone have a comment?"

Riley shook her head quickly. "No, Coach."

"Good," Coach said. "Warm up outside the arena door, then enter one at a time so we do not trample each other. Let us make the most of this snow day."

The girls finished tacking up. Emma wrapped Knightfall in a cooler and clipped on his reins. He walked beside her with a steady rhythm that always soothed her nerves. She patted his neck.

"You ready, boy?"

He nudged her lightly.

The indoor arena door stood open just enough to hear muffled voices and the rhythmic thud of hooves. Emma saw glimpses of other riders circling at the far end. The air inside shimmered with warmth, but the atmosphere hummed with tension. Winter riding had begun in earnest.

Riley appeared at her side with Ruby, who continued prancing in place.

"She needs to get in there," Riley muttered. "Before she explodes."

Zoey joined on Emma's other side, Daisy walking more politely but still alert.

"I am trying to stay positive," Zoey whispered. "But I have already seen three near crashes in the last ten minutes."

Emma inhaled slowly, trying to summon the calm that she felt earlier in the morning. It was harder now. The indoor felt louder, tighter, and more crowded than she expected. Winter afternoons brought a mix of riders from different age groups, and skill levels varied wildly. Some riders could hold a straight line. Others wandered like lost sheep.

Coach motioned them through the doorway. "One at a time. Emma first. Zoey second. Riley, wait for my signal."

Emma mounted Knightfall, adjusted her gloves, and guided him into the arena.

The warmth hit her immediately, a welcome wave compared to the cold outside. The sand beneath Knightfall's hooves felt freshly dragged, but the lines from the earlier lessons were still visible. The arena lights cast a soft yellow hue across the space.

"Track left in walk," Coach called.

Knightfall stepped forward calmly, ears flicking between Emma's quiet encouragement and the commotion around them. Riders passed in both directions, some more confidently than others. A pony in the corner jigged sideways, startling its rider. A tall bay gelding lumbered past, snorting with impatience.

Emma guided Knightfall around the perimeter while Zoey entered behind her. Daisy moved beautifully, her neck arched with natural grace. Zoey gave a small wave.

Then Riley entered.

Ruby surged forward the moment her hooves hit the sand. Riley shortened her reins quickly, muttering warnings under her breath.

"Do not even think about it," Riley said to Ruby.

Ruby snorted loudly, tossing her head high.

Coach blew her whistle once. "Riley, get her bending. Inside leg. Do not let her barrel forward."

Riley tried. Ruby responded by shaking her mane and powering ahead like a small runaway train.

"Do we need hazard lights for Ruby?" Zoey whispered to Emma.

Emma coughed to hide her laugh.

Riley heard them anyway. "I can hear you two," she snapped.

Zoey held up her hands. "We are just making sure you are okay."

"I am fine," Riley said sharply. "Ruby is the one acting possessed."

Despite the bickering, the girls tried to warm up in an orderly pattern. Coach directed them through circles and serpentines to keep the horses focused. It worked for a while. Knightfall softened into his trot. Daisy stretched her stride, graceful as always. Ruby settled for exactly twelve seconds before launching forward again.

The crowding grew worse once another lesson joined. Fifteen horses moved through the space, weaving between cones and poles set up for pattern work. The footing churned under the hooves, and dust rose under the lights.

Coach tried to maintain order. "Lefts have right of way. Watch your spacing. That is not spacing. Move out of each other's lines."

A younger rider lost her balance at one point, and her pony veered sideways directly into Daisy's path. Zoey pulled Daisy up short, just in time.

"Sorry," the younger girl squeaked.

"It is okay," Zoey said warmly, though Emma saw her jaw tighten.

Emma took another lap around the ring. Knightfall focused mostly, though he was starting to get irritated with a pony whose tail kept swishing into his face. Emma steered wider to avoid the distraction.

The tension in the indoor grew with every passing minute. The noise. The closeness. The horses growing restless. Emma felt it too. Winter riding might have charm, but it also had pressure.

Then it happened.

Riley was cantering Ruby on the outside track when Ruby spotted a dangling tarp outside the arena window. The wind had caught it, making it flap like a bird trying to escape. Ruby threw her head up and shot sideways, nearly colliding with Zoey.

Zoey yanked Daisy out of the way at the last second. Even so, Daisy stumbled a step. Zoey gasped, grabbing her mane to steady herself.

"Watch it," Zoey said, her voice higher than usual.

Riley's face flushed bright red. "I did not do anything. Ruby spooked."

"You were too close," Zoey replied.

"I was not," Riley snapped. "You cut in."

Emma intervened instantly. "Riley, Zoey, stop. Both of you. It was an accident."

Zoey looked hurt. Riley looked furious.

Coach strode toward them, her boots thudding across the sand. "What happened?"

Zoey opened her mouth first. "Ruby swerved and almost hit us."

Riley scowled. "Because Daisy drifted into our line."

"I did not drift," Zoey fired back.

Emma winced. This was exactly the kind of tension winter riding created. The indoor magnified every mistake, every emotion.

Coach held up a hand. "Enough. Both of you. No one is blaming anyone. Horses spook. Riders try their best. That is reality. What matters is how you recover and communicate. And right now the communication is terrible."

Riley stared at her reins, chest rising and falling quickly. Zoey looked down too, her lip pressed tight.

Emma watched both of them. Something fragile was stretching thin again. Fall had cracked their friendship. Winter was pressing hard on the same fault line.

Coach pointed between them. "You two are partners in this barn. If you cannot ride near each other safely, you should not be in the same arena until you talk."

Zoey swallowed. Riley gritted her teeth.

Emma stepped closer, hoping to ease the tension, but Coach signaled her to stay back.

"Cool down your horses," Coach said firmly. "Then walk them out in the main barn aisle. We will try again after a reset."

The three girls nodded and separated.

Emma walked Knightfall toward the quieter side of the ring. The soft sound of his hooves helped settle her breathing. She glanced toward Zoey and Riley. They walked in opposite directions, their shoulders stiff, their mouths pressed tight.

Emma felt a twinge of worry. Winter was just beginning. There would be weeks of crowding and indoor chaos. If Zoey and Riley cracked this early, the season would be long and difficult.

Still, she knew friendships at Saddle Creek had weathered worse storms than this. And winter storms, no matter how loud they raged, always passed.

For now, she focused on letting Knightfall stretch his neck and relax. The next part of training would begin soon, and she wanted to meet it with a clear mind.

Beyond the arena windows, the snow thickened, swirling faster, almost like the sky itself was stirring up a warning. Emma did not know it yet, but tonight's storm would bring more than cold winds. It would test their patience, their teamwork, and their courage.

And it would pull them all together in ways they could not yet imagine.

Because winter at Saddle Creek had only begun.

Chapter Three

By the next afternoon the snow had settled into deep, soft drifts that curved along the fences like pale waves. Saddle Creek looked quiet from the outside, but inside the barn the air pulsed with noise and motion. Winter had a way of squeezing everyone into the same space, and it did not always bring out the best in people.

Emma stood in the aisle fastening Knightfall's girth while the afternoon group gathered. Hooves clinked on concrete. Riders spoke over one another. Somewhere down the row, a pony scratched its rump against a stall door, rattling the latch.

"Full house again," Zoey said, appearing at Emma's side with Daisy in tow. She wore the same snowberry beanie, slightly crooked over her curls. "Coach has three groups overlapping today. The indoor is going to feel like a crowded supermarket at five o clock."

Emma gave a small smile. "At least we are getting a lot of saddle time."

Zoey shrugged. "True. That spring clinic rumor is not going to prepare for itself."

The reminder fluttered in Emma's chest like a small spark. The clinic was still only a maybe, but Coach had mentioned having a call with someone that morning. Already, Emma could not help imagining a famous trainer in their little arena, watching Knightfall, pointing out ways they could grow.

"Do you think Coach got any news?" Emma asked.

"Not yet," Zoey said. "She said she would tell us when there is something solid. She does not want us building castles in the air before she signs any forms."

"Fair," Emma said.

Farther down the aisle, Riley led Ruby out of her stall. Ruby's ears flicked and her muscles bunched under her coat as if she were made of springs. Riley's jaw was tight, her braid pulled so neatly that not a single strand escaped. She had been quieter than usual all day, answering questions with single words, moving as if the world annoyed her simply by existing.

Zoey watched her for a moment. "There she is. Miss Winter Sunshine."

"Zoey," Emma said in a warning tone.

Zoey lifted her hands. "I did not say anything to her."

"No, but she can hear you," Emma replied.

Riley glanced in their direction, eyes narrowing slightly. She did not come over. Instead she clipped Ruby in and began brushing with quick, sharp strokes.

Emma felt a familiar knot of worry. Yesterday's near collision in the arena had ended with Coach separating them and insisting on a cool down. No one had really talked it through after that. They had untacked, gone home, and pretended the air did not crackle around them.

Now the tension floated in the barn like invisible fog.

"Maybe we should say something before the lesson?" Emma suggested quietly.

Zoey bit her lip. "Like what? Sorry your horse spooked and nearly took my knee off?"

"Maybe just check in," Emma said. "You know how she gets

when winter starts. And the medal final still sits in the back of her mind."

Zoey sighed. "Fine. I can be mature." She wrinkled her nose. "At least for five minutes."

Emma smiled. "That is all we need."

They finished tacking up in silence. Knightfall stood patiently as Emma fastened his bridle. Daisy shifted, eager to move. Ruby pawed the ground and snorted.

Just as they were about to lead their horses out, Coach appeared in the aisle, tugging off her gloves.

"Listen up, everyone," she called. "The indoor is beyond full. We are going to run a pattern lesson to keep things organized. That means strict tracks and clear communication. This is not the time to show off moves you saw on the internet. Follow the plan, and we can all leave with our limbs intact."

A ripple of laughter moved through the riders.

Coach continued. "Older riders on the outside track. Younger ones inside the cones. If anyone starts treating the arena like a race-track, I will have you mucking stalls until summer. Clear?"

A chorus of "Yes, Coach" echoed back.

Coach's gaze landed briefly on Riley, Zoey, and Emma. For a moment, Emma thought she might pull them aside. Instead, Coach gave a small nod, as if trusting them to handle themselves.

"Mount up in the warm up area," she finished. "Enter in pairs when I call you."

Emma led Knightfall toward the indoor. The hallway to the arena felt even narrower today, crowded with horses and riders waiting their turn. The walls seemed closer, the air thicker. Steam rose from horse coats, fogging the windows.

As they waited, Zoey took a breath. "Alright. I am going in," she whispered. She left Daisy with her mother at the doorway and walked back toward Riley.

Emma stayed with Knightfall, pretending to fuss with his stirrups while her ears strained to hear.

"Hey," Zoey said softly when she reached Riley.

Riley kept brushing a fleck of dust from Ruby's mane that was not really there. "What."

Zoey forced a small smile. "I just wanted to say, about yesterday. I know Ruby did not mean to freak out. I was a little sharp with my words."

Riley's shoulders stiffened. "You think."

Zoey hesitated. "I did not want to make it worse. I was scared Daisy would get hurt. That is all."

Riley stopped brushing and looked at her, eyes cool but wounded. "You think I wanted Ruby to slam into you? You think I was having fun up there?"

"No," Zoey said quickly. "That is not what I meant."

"Because it sounded like you thought it was my fault," Riley went on. Her voice stayed level, but Emma could hear the crack underneath. "Like I am the only one who messes up."

Zoey blinked. "I never said that."

"You did not have to," Riley replied. "Everyone looks at Ruby and me like we are the problem every time something goes wrong."

"That is not true," Zoey protested.

Riley snorted. "Sure."

Emma stepped forward with Knightfall, pulling up alongside them. "Hey," she said gently. "Coach is calling us. Maybe we can talk after the lesson?"

Riley shrugged, but the gesture looked more like a flinch. "Whatever. Let us just get this over with."

They mounted when Coach called their names. Emma swung into the saddle and settled her weight, feeling Knightfall's muscles shift beneath her. Zoey mounted Daisy, adjusting her reins with practiced precision. Riley climbed onto Ruby, who immediately tried to bounce into trot. Riley held her back with a muttered warning.

Inside, the arena buzzed with activity. Cones outlined an inner oval track where younger riders walked and trotted under the watchful eye of an assistant instructor. The outer track belonged to the older riders, circling in a steady stream. Poles lay on the ground in one corner for bending patterns. At the far end, a line of small cross rails waited.

Coach stood near the center with a whistle around her neck and a clipboard in hand. She looked like a traffic controller, eyes scanning every movement.

"Join the outer track at the quarter line," she called to Emma's group. "Left direction. Keep a safe distance. That does not mean half a horse length. Give each other room."

Emma guided Knightfall into the flow. Daisy settled behind them, steady and elegant. Ruby followed, tossing her head, her hooves punching the sand a little harder than needed. Riley adjusted her reins, jaw set.

"Walk until I call trot," Coach instructed.

They circled once, twice. Knightfall stretched his neck, ears flicking. Emma focused on her breathing, using the rhythm of his steps to steady her thoughts.

"Track left, trot," Coach called.

Emma squeezed lightly and Knightfall picked up a smooth trot. Daisy followed suit, her strides matching almost perfectly. Ruby leaped into a trot with too much energy, forcing Riley to half halt.

"Riley, soften your hands but stay firm with your leg," Coach said. "You are stopping the energy instead of shaping it."

"I am trying," Riley replied tightly.

The first few minutes went well enough. They trotted along the outer track, weaving around slower horses, calling out "inside" or "passing" as needed. Occasionally, a younger rider drifted too far out from the cone line, and an older rider had to adjust quickly.

Emma passed the mirror and caught a glimpse of herself and Knightfall. They looked more balanced than they had last winter. That gave her a quiet thrill. Progress did not always roar. Sometimes it whispered.

"Prepare for a three loop serpentine," Coach called to the older group. "Use the full width between outer track and inner cones. Do not run over the small ones. They break. And then I am sad."

A few riders chuckled.

Coach pointed at Emma. "You lead the pattern. Zoey behind you. Riley, third position. Others follow in order."

Emma swallowed. Leading meant everyone watched her line. If she misjudged the spacing, the whole pattern might crumble. She felt Knightfall's ears flick back, waiting for her cue. She straightened her shoulders.

"Okay, we can do this," she murmured.

On Coach's signal, Emma steered Knightfall off the rail, guiding him in a smooth curve toward the first loop. Daisy followed faithfully. Behind them, Ruby snorted and tossed her head, but Riley kept her in line.

The first loop went well. They curved back across the center, then out toward the far side of the arena. The younger riders inside the cone oval kept trotting in smaller circles, eyes wide as the older group moved around them.

The second loop got tricky. Another horse ahead of them hesitated, and the spacing shrank. Emma had to adjust quickly, asking Knightfall to shorten slightly. He obeyed, though his ears flicked uncertainly.

"Good correction, Emma," Coach called.

Daisy adjusted easily behind them. Ruby did not.

As they started the third loop, Ruby surged forward, frustrated by the repeated slowdowns. Riley fought to steady her. For a moment, they were too close to Daisy's hindquarters.

"Riley, give more space," Coach called sharply.

"I am trying," Riley gritted out.

"Circle if you cannot maintain distance," Coach replied. "Safety first."

Riley hesitated. Ruby took that moment to dive to the inside, cutting across part of Zoey's line. Daisy tossed her head, offended. Zoey sat up straight, eyes wide.

"Ruby!" Riley gasped.

"Watch it," Zoey snapped. Her voice cracked with frayed nerves. "You keep cutting in."

"I am not doing it on purpose," Riley shot back.

"You always say that," Zoey retorted. "Every time."

"Then maybe stop riding in front of me if you think I am so dangerous," Riley said, her cheeks flushed.

"Girls," Coach warned, but the word dropped into air that already felt electric.

Their horses kept moving. The pattern continued, but the focus was gone. Emma did her best to hold Knightfall's line, but her attention kept sliding backward toward her friends.

When they reached the rail again, Coach ordered them back to a working trot on the outer track. The rhythm returned, yet the tension nicked at the edges of every stride.

"Older group, prepare for canter transitions on the long sides only," Coach called. "Walk the short sides. That should help with crowding."

Emma took a steadying breath. Knightfall was more reliable in canter these days, but the crowded indoor made her careful. She did not want to repeat any of the chaos from fall.

"At the letter A, Emma and Knightfall canter. At C, return to trot," Coach said. "Zoey and Daisy follow one marker behind. Riley and Ruby, you wait one long side and then join."

They approached A. Emma squeezed with her outside leg and gave a kiss. Knightfall rose into canter, smooth and rolling. She kept him on the rail, focusing on straightness.

At C, she brought him back to trot. Daisy followed the same pattern, elegant and measured. They walked the short side while Coach watched.

"Good," Coach called. "Now Riley, your turn. At E, ask Ruby to canter. Give her direction before she gives you chaos."

Riley set her jaw and nodded. As they approached E, she gathered her reins and asked. Ruby leaped into canter with a powerful surge, throwing her hindquarters slightly toward the inside. Riley fought to keep her on the track.

"Inside leg," Coach reminded.

"I am trying," Riley snapped.

Ruby barreled down the long side, ears pinned at a horse in the middle of the ring who was practicing transitions. Riley wrestled to keep her balanced.

At the end of the long side, Riley sat deep and pulled. Ruby dropped into a choppy trot and then almost to a halt, tossing her head.

"Do not yank," Coach said firmly. "Breathe. Ride her forward into the downward transition. She needs a place to go."

"I know," Riley said, but her voice sounded brittle.

They tried again. And again. Each attempt went a little better, but the frustration piled up like snowdrifts in the corners. The other riders kept circling, some doing fine, some struggling. One boy on a chunky paint horse kept cutting inside without looking, forcing others to adjust around him. Twice, a younger rider drifted out from the cones. Coach's corrections came faster and sharper.

Finally, it happened.

During a canter set, Ruby saw the flapping tarp outside the window again. A gust of wind lifted it, making it slap the fence. Ruby startled sideways toward the inner track.

Daisy was there.

Zoey tried to move out of the way, but the space was too tight. Ruby's shoulder bumped Daisy's hindquarters. Daisy kicked out immediately, more in surprise than anger. The impact was not hard, but it jolted both horses.

Zoey grabbed Daisy's mane to steady herself. Riley gasped and yanked on the reins. Ruby flung her head, hopping once on her hind legs.

The entire flow of the lesson stuttered. Several riders pulled up. Someone yelped. A pony shied at the commotion.

Coach blew her whistle, a sharp sound that cut through the noise.

"Walk," she barked. "Everyone walk. Now."

The horses slowed. The ring filled with uneven breathing and the shuffling of hooves.

Coach turned to Zoey and Riley. "Are you two alright?"

Zoey nodded shakily. "I am fine. Daisy is fine. Just surprised."

Riley blinked fast. "I am fine. Ruby is just being ridiculous."

"She is not ridiculous," Zoey burst out. "She is dangerous when you do not pay attention."

Riley's head snapped around. "Excuse me?"

"You keep getting too close," Zoey said. Her face had gone pale, but her eyes glittered. "This is the second time in two days. You cut across my line again."

"I did not cut across," Riley said, her voice rising. "The tarp scared her."

"You know she hates that tarp," Zoey replied. "You know she overreacts to everything, and you still gallop her down the long side like a runaway freight train."

The entire arena had gone quiet. Even the younger riders on the inner track had stopped trotting and were watching with wide, uncertain eyes.

Emma's heart thudded in her ears. She wanted to intervene, but she did not know how to do it without making either of them feel cornered.

"Zoey," Emma said softly. "Maybe we can talk about this out of the saddle."

Zoey did not look at her. She kept her gaze fixed on Riley. "I am tired of almost getting run over."

"Maybe stop hogging the best lines, then," Riley snapped. Her cheeks were flaming now. "You act like this arena belongs to you and Daisy. The rest of us are just obstacles."

"That is not fair," Zoey said. Her voice shook.

"What is not fair," Riley shot back, "is that every time something goes wrong, everyone looks at me like it is my fault. Ruby spooks, and suddenly I am the careless one. I mess up a distance, and suddenly I do not care about anyone else in the ring. You do not get blamed when Daisy shies. You do not get sideways looks when she jumps too big. It is always me."

"Riley," Emma tried again. "No one thinks you do not care."

"Yes they do," Riley said hotly. "You do not understand. You two always look so perfect. Everyone loves watching Daisy float around. Everyone loves how Knightfall looks like he belongs in a magazine now that he has decided not to refuse everything. I am tired of being the one everyone expects to cause trouble."

Zoey's mouth fell open. "You think I feel perfect out there? I am terrified half the time that I am going to mess Daisy up. Coach puts us in front because she thinks we can help set the pace. That is pressure too."

"At least she trusts you with it," Riley replied. "She only trusts me to be the example of what not to do."

"That is not true," Emma said quickly, but her words felt too small for the storm brewing beside her.

Coach had moved closer, but for the moment she let the words spill. Sometimes, Emma knew, Coach believed the truth had to come out before anyone could start mending it.

Riley looked from Zoey to Emma, her eyes shining with more than anger now. Something raw and old sat there too.

"You know what I am really tired of?" Riley said. Her voice dropped, but somehow it carried just as far. "I am tired of always being the one who pushes myself in ways I hate. Shows that make me sick to my stomach. Medal classes that never feel like they fit me. Long summer trail days that go on forever until my legs feel numb and my brain will not stop screaming that something bad is going to happen. I never want those again. Those long summer trail days? They are the worst. I hate them. I never want to do them ever again."

The words hung in the air, heavy and strange.

Emma felt a shiver that had nothing to do with the cold. She knew Riley liked speed and competition. She knew Riley loved the feeling of a powerful horse under her. But she had never heard her talk about trail rides like that, with that much intensity. It was as if the thought of endless summer miles weighed on her chest like a stone.

Zoey blinked, thrown off balance. "Riley, if you hate them that much, why do you keep signing up?"

"Because that is what good riders do," Riley snapped. "They push through. They pretend they love every part of it. They do not admit when something scares them or bores them or twists their stomach into knots."

Emma saw it then. Beneath the anger, Riley was afraid. Not just of Ruby's spooks or tight winter arenas, but of being left behind, of not measuring up, of disappointing people who believed she was fearless.

"Riley," Emma said quietly, "you are allowed to not love every part of this."

Riley's jaw clenched. "Tell that to everyone who will blame me if I quit a class or skip a trail ride. Tell that to the parents who pay for lessons and shows and expect smiles in every photo. Tell that to the riders who think long summer trail days are magical and healing. Some of us just feel trapped."

Zoey swallowed. Her anger softened, replaced by uncertainty. "I did not know you felt like that."

"Maybe if you listened instead of assuming I enjoy being the problem, you would," Riley said.

Zoey flinched.

That was enough for Coach.

"Alright," Coach said, her voice firm but not harsh. "That is where we stop. Walk your horses out on the rail. Eyes up. Hands quiet. Breathe."

The girls obeyed, though the tension still hummed around them. Knightfall moved forward under Emma, his ears swivelling as if he could sense the emotional storm as clearly as any physical one.

Coach walked alongside them for a minute, watching their body language as much as their horses.

"Everyone else," Coach called to the ring, "you can pick up a relaxed trot on the inside track if you feel comfortable. Keep things light. No more patterns for now."

The rest of the riders eased back into motion, glancing occasionally at the trio on the rail. A few younger riders whispered to each other, curiosity and worry mixed in their expressions.

Coach lowered her voice when she spoke to Emma, Zoey, and Riley. "You three are not going to solve this in the middle of a crowded lesson. But you are also not going to pretend nothing happened."

Emma nodded, throat tight.

Zoey stared straight ahead. Riley looked at the far corner of the arena, as if focusing anywhere else might keep her from falling apart.

"We will finish this lesson at the walk," Coach said. "I want you focusing on your horses and your own breathing. After you untack, you are coming to the lounge with me. We will talk. No yelling. No blaming. Just facts and feelings. Understood?"

"Yes, Coach," they murmured.

"Good," she said. "Now walk on. Give the horses a chance to relax. They did not start this argument."

Emma let Knightfall stretch his neck. She focused on the steady swing of his shoulders, the softness of his mouth on the bit. Being in the saddle helped her think more clearly. Emotions still churned, but they had a rhythm now.

Zoey stroked Daisy's neck, her eyes shining. Riley stared ahead, fingers twitching on the reins, then finally softened them, letting Ruby march forward with a little sigh.

The rest of the lesson passed in a quiet haze. Coach kept instructions simple. Transitions. Big circles. No complex patterns. The atmosphere shifted from crackling to heavy, like the sky before a storm breaks.

Outside, the wind had started to howl around the barn, rattling the eaves. Snow whipped past the windows in sudden gusts. The tarp slapped and fluttered, but Coach had moved a horse trailer in front of it earlier, muting the sound.

Emma noticed the change in the weather with a faint chill of recognition. Storms did not only come in the sky. They came between people too.

When Coach finally called the end of the lesson, the girls dismounted in silence. They led their horses out of the arena and down the narrow hallway. The wall of photos watched them pass, riders from years ago frozen in moments of triumph and joy.

In the barn aisle, Emma loosened Knightfall's girth with careful fingers. Her hands shook despite her efforts to stay calm.

"You okay?" Harper asked quietly from the next cross tie, where she was unbuckling Fern's bridle. Harper had joined the outer track halfway through the lesson, staying out of the argument but seeing enough to understand the tension.

"I do not know yet," Emma admitted.

Harper nodded. "I am here if you want to talk afterward."

"Thanks," Emma said.

She slid the saddle off Knightfall's back, letting the warm steam rise into the cool barn air. Zoey worked in silence beside her, folding Daisy's pad with neat precision. Riley pulled Ruby's tack off quickly, movements fast enough that the girth clanged against the saddle rack.

The storm outside roared louder now, wind shoving against the barn walls, snow scraping across the roof. Inside, everything felt strangely still. Even the horses seemed to sense that something important had shifted, though no one knew yet whether it would break them apart or make them stronger.

When the last girth was hung and the last blanket fastened, Coach appeared at the end of the aisle.

"Emma. Zoey. Riley," she said. "Lounge. Ten minutes."

Her tone left no room for argument.

Zoey swallowed hard. Riley did not look up. Emma gave Knightfall one last stroke along the neck, drawing courage from the familiar feel of his coat.

"I will be back," she whispered.

Knightfall breathed softly against her sleeve, as if he understood.

As the three girls walked toward the lounge together, none of them spoke. Their boots thudded on the worn wooden floor. The wind howled outside. Somewhere in the rafters, a loose rope tapped lightly against the beams, counting out the seconds.

Winter at Saddle Creek had always been about learning to endure cold and darkness with the warmth of friends and horses. Now, for the first time, Emma wondered whether their friendships could weather this kind of storm.

She hoped so. Because somewhere beyond the winter and all its crowded, frustrating lessons lay a spring that promised new chances. And beyond that, a summer that would test Riley in ways even she could not yet imagine.

For now, though, everything narrowed to one small room at the front of the barn, three chairs, one coach, and a conversation that might decide how the rest of the season unfolded.

Chapter Four

The lounge at Saddle Creek felt unusually warm compared to the hallway outside. The radiator along the wall rattled softly, fighting the rising cold as the storm gathered strength. Emma sat in one of the wooden chairs, Knightfall's lead rope curled around her fists even though he was back in his stall. Holding it made her feel steady. Safe. Grounded.

Riley sat opposite her, slouched in her chair with arms folded tight across her chest. Zoey sat between them, her posture straighter than usual, knees pressed together, hands clasped so tightly her knuckles had gone pale.

Coach closed the lounge door and took a seat facing the girls. She did not sigh or scold or shift impatiently. She simply sat with them, creating a quiet space where everything felt less sharp.

"You three matter to this barn," Coach began, her voice calm. "And that means your friendships matter too. Winter puts pressure on all of us. Indoor crowds. Fresh horses. Limited space. It amplifies small problems until they feel huge." She folded her hands. "But none of that excuses hurting each other."

Emma nodded. Zoey stared down. Riley blinked hard.

"Emma," Coach said. "Start us off."

Emma took a breath. "Ruby spooked. Daisy reacted. I think we were all tense already. The arena was loud and crowded. The argument got bigger than the moment."

Coach nodded once. "Zoey?"

Zoey hesitated. "I did not mean to accuse Riley. It just scared me when Ruby came across Daisy again. I reacted without thinking. It felt like I had to defend myself before anyone blamed me."

Riley's shoulders softened a little at that.

"And Riley?" Coach asked.

Riley stared at her gloved hands. "Ruby is a lot in winter. I thought I had her under control. When she jumped sideways again I felt embarrassed and angry at myself. I felt like everyone was waiting for me to mess up." Her voice cracked. "I did not want to explode like that. But I felt cornered."

Coach listened without judgment. "Thank you for being honest."

Outside, wind pressed against the siding with a long groan. Snow swept past the windows in fast waves.

Coach looked between them. "Riding is supposed to make us stronger, not tear us apart. You all needed to say these things, but you also need to hear each other."

Zoey looked at Riley, her eyes gentler now. "I am sorry I snapped at you. I got scared. I was too sharp."

Riley swallowed. "I am sorry too. I know Ruby is unpredictable sometimes. I need to be more aware. And I should not have yelled."

Emma felt tension ease from the room like air leaving an overfilled balloon.

Coach nodded with approval. "Good. You will still need to work on communication, but this is a start. Now, head back to the barn. Ginger tea in the kettle. Hot chocolate mix next to it."

As the girls stepped out of the lounge, the hallway lights flickered for a moment. The storm must have been hitting harder now.

Emma checked her phone. "The forecast says the wind chill is dropping fast."

Zoey shivered even inside her coat. "Great."

They made their way back toward the stalls when a burst of footsteps echoed behind them. Harper appeared, arms full of fleece blankets and a grin that nearly split her face.

"Hold on," Harper said breathlessly. "My mom just called. She said the roads are getting sketchy and the storm might cut the power. She said the barn is safer than the drive home if it gets worse. And then she asked Coach if we could do a winter sleepover here tonight."

Zoey gasped. "Wait. A real barn sleepover? During a storm?"

"Yes," Harper said, practically bouncing. "My mom said she would drop off sleeping bags and snacks. She thinks it would be fun."

Emma's heart fluttered with excitement. "We would be here if the horses get restless. And it would be warm in the loft."

Riley hesitated. "I do not know. Storms at the barn feel creepy sometimes. The wind makes weird noises."

Zoey nudged her. "We will bring fairy lights. And popcorn. And you will not be alone."

Riley's mouth twitched into the beginnings of a smile. "Fine. But Ruby is not allowed near my sleeping bag."

Harper giggled. "Deal."

Coach walked up behind them, shaking her head with a small but amused sigh. "If your parents approve, and if the storm continues the way it is going, we will keep you here. I expect quiet hours after ten and respectful behavior around the horses." She paused. "And I choose the movie. None of your ghost horse nonsense."

Zoey pressed a hand to her heart. "We would never."

Riley raised an eyebrow. "We absolutely would."

Emma laughed, the sound lifting the last of the tension from the air.

They hurried back to their stalls to brush out manes, fill hay nets, and check blankets again. Knightfall leaned into Emma's hands as she brushed his neck, his eyes soft in the warm barn light.

"You might hear us giggling all night," she whispered to him. "Try to pretend we are not embarrassing."

He blew warm air against her cheek, which counted as a yes.

Across the aisle, Zoey hummed to Daisy, brushing away bits of arena dust. Riley leaned her forehead against Ruby's neck, her expression calmer than it had been all day.

Harper darted in and out of stalls, checking water buckets, setting up extra bedding, and announcing new ideas for the sleepover every thirty seconds. "We can hang blankets between the rafters. And we can make cocoa on Coach's stove. And we can play that game where you guess the horse by the sound of its hoofbeats."

"Harper," Zoey laughed, "slow down before you run out of oxygen."

"I am just excited," Harper said, cheeks glowing. "Storm nights feel magical."

Emma looked out the small window at the end of the aisle. Snow swirled thick and fast, pushed sideways by the wind. Trees along the fence line bent under the weight of it. The sky had gone from soft gray to dark steel.

Winter had teeth tonight.

But inside the barn, the lights glowed warm on polished tack and fresh hay. Horses chewed peacefully. Friends moved in an easy rhythm around each other again.

For the first time that afternoon, Emma felt a deep sense of belonging settle in her chest. Whatever the storm brought, they would face it together.

The laughter. The fear. The adventure.

And the horses would always be at the center of it.

Saddle Creek was home.

And tonight, home would become a place of stories they would remember for years.

Chapter Five

The storm arrived slowly at first, like a shy guest testing the door. Soft flakes drifted past the barn windows as the girls carried their pillows and sleeping bags up the loft ladder. By the time Emma reached the top, the world outside had blurred into white. Snow pressed thick against the glass panes, trickling in swirling patterns that looked almost like falling stars.

The loft smelled of hay, wood, and the faint sweetness of molasses grain. The rafters curved overhead like the ribs of a giant ship. Everything felt cozy and warm, especially once Harper unrolled a string of battery fairy lights across one beam.

"There," Harper said proudly. "Instant magic."

Zoey dropped her sleeping bag in the middle of the floor. "It looks like a winter postcard in here."

Emma set her blanket beside Knightfall's stall below. She wished she could see him from the loft, but the rails blocked the view except through a few small gaps. She knew he would be fine. Knightfall handled storms better than some of the others. Still, she paused to listen for the soft rumble of his breath from below.

Riley tossed her bag down with a grunt. "This is going to be cramped."

Zoey nudged her lightly. "That is part of the adventure."

Riley muttered something that sounded like maybe, but she did not argue as she sat cross legged and began arranging her blanket.

Coach carried a kettle up the ladder next, shaking snow from her shoulders. "Hot water. Choose cocoa or tea. No one touches the kettle without me watching this time."

Zoey gasped in mock offense. "That was a single incident."

Coach raised an eyebrow. "A single incident that ended with three burnt marshmallows and one melted plastic cup."

The girls burst out laughing.

Emma accepted a cup from Coach and sat with it cupped between her hands. The warmth sank into her fingers. The smell of chocolate drifted through the loft, mixing with the soft sounds of horses shifting below them.

Daisy gave a quiet whicker. Ruby pawed her bedding once, testing it. Fern snorted. Knightfall breathed slowly, steady as a tide.

For a while, the girls simply talked.

Harper told a story about the time her pony chewed through an entire lead rope while she was distracted by a butterfly. Zoey shared the tale of Daisy's first show, when the mare backed out of the trailer halfway and refused to go forward until someone produced peppermints. Riley confessed that Ruby once escaped her pasture by belly crawling under a fence board, which made all of them howl with laughter.

"Ruby has too much confidence," Zoey said between giggles.

Riley rolled her eyes but looked proud. "She knows she is special."

Emma leaned back on her elbows, smiling at the familiar rhythms of her friends' voices. The earlier tension felt far away now. The cocoa, the glow of fairy lights, the shared stories, all of it smoothed their edges until they felt whole again.

Harper rummaged in her backpack and produced a bag of caramel popcorn. "Snacks for survival."

Zoey reached for a handful. "People in winter movies always have popcorn."

Riley grabbed some too. "Movies are lying. In real storms people have canned food and stress."

"We have popcorn and stress," Zoey countered.

"Fair point," Riley said.

They talked until the light outside faded completely and the windows turned black. The fairy lights cast a soft glow across the rafters. The wind groaned occasionally, pushing snow against the siding in heavy waves. It was the kind of sound that made Emma think of stories her grandmother used to tell about forest spirits and winter wolves. Not scary, exactly. Just wild.

Coach climbed the ladder one more time with her phone in hand. "Weather update," she said.

The girls sat up straighter.

Coach checked the screen. "The storm is picking up speed. Wind gusts will reach dangerous levels soon. Roads are already closing. I told your parents you will stay here for the night. Everyone is fine with it."

Zoey clapped once. Riley sighed with relief. Harper curled tighter into her blanket. Emma exhaled slowly. It felt good to have the decision made for them.

Coach unplugged the fairy lights and plugged them into a small battery pack. "Power might go out. Stay calm if it does. The generator sometimes acts up, but we will handle it."

She pointed toward the aisle below. "Keep your voices down. Horses are sensitive in storms."

"Yes, Coach," they chorused.

Coach gave them one last look before heading down the ladder. "No ghost stories after ten. I do not want Daisy panicking because someone thinks they heard hoofprints from beyond."

Zoey grinned. "We would never do that."

Emma snorted. "We absolutely would do that."

The girls erupted into more quiet laughter.

But only a few minutes later, the mood shifted.

It happened gradually. The wind rose in pitch, pressing so hard on the walls that the rafters trembled. Snow pelted the windows in sheets. A long moan traveled across the roof, vibrating the boards under their sleeping bags.

Then they heard the horses.

A sudden thump. Then another. A squeal from the far end. Hooves scraping in a stall. The sound of someone pawing hard, as if agitated.

Emma sat up fast. "That was Knightfall."

Riley was already on her feet. "Ruby is moving around."

Zoey pressed her hands flat against the floorboards. "Daisy is pacing."

Harper peered over the edge of the loft. "Fern is restless too."

Emma's heart pinched. Storms were not new, but horses always reacted differently to them. Some stayed calm. Others grew anxious. The noise, the vibrations, the sudden gusts, all of it could unsettle even the steadiest mare.

A loud crack of wind slapped the side of the barn. The loft lights flickered once, twice, then steadied.

Zoey's eyes widened. "Was that the power...?"

Another crack. This one louder.

Emma felt the air shift around them, colder now, sharper.

Coach called from below. "Girls, stay put for the moment."

But they were already gathering their blankets, crawling toward the railing to see better.

The horses shuffled and snorted in their stalls. Ruby stomped hard enough that the bedding rustled. Knightfall tossed his head, shaking his mane. Daisy backed up to the far corner of her stall, ears flicked backward.

Emma's pulse quickened. "We should go down. They are scared."

Coach reappeared below them with a flashlight in hand. "Stay in the loft until I check the generator. If the power goes, I need you safe and away from the horses. Do not come down unless I call for you."

The girls exchanged uncertain glances, but Emma saw the worry etched in Coach's posture. This was not one of their usual winter squalls. This storm had force.

"Okay," Emma said quietly. "We will stay."

Coach nodded firmly. "Good. I will be right back."

She disappeared toward the back hallway.

The girls gathered closer to the railing, the loft suddenly feeling far too high above the shifting horses below. The wind roared again, rattling the eaves so hard that a faint vibration ran up the ladder.

Zoey hugged her knees. "I do not like the sound of that."

Riley stood with her arms crossed, eyes locked on Ruby's stall. "She is going to jump out if this keeps up."

Harper whispered, "Do horses know when storms are dangerous?"

"Yes," Emma said softly. "They feel it before we do."

The lights flickered again.

A cold silence filled the loft.

Then, with a soft sigh like the barn taking one long breath, everything went dark.

The girls froze.

Only the sound of the wind, the shuffling of hooves, and the faint shake of rafters filled the air.

Emma inhaled slowly.

This was no longer a cozy sleepover.

This was the beginning of a night they would never forget.

Chapter Six

The darkness arrived all at once, steady and complete. One second the fairy lights glowed softly across the loft. The next, the entire barn seemed to exhale into shadow. Emma blinked in the pitch black, waiting for her eyes to adjust, but the night pressed in too quickly.

Below them, a horse let out a sharp snort. Another stomped. The soft shuffle of hooves grew louder as the storm rattled the siding again.

Zoey whispered, "Emma...?"

"I am here," Emma whispered back, reaching out until her hand touched Zoey's sleeve.

Riley's voice came next, low but steady. "Everyone breathe. Do not panic."

Harper let out a shaky exhale. "The power really went out."

A faint beam of light suddenly flickered below. Coach's flashlight wobbled across the aisle, illuminating pieces of tack, the rafters above, and the restless movements of horses standing in their stalls.

"Girls," Coach called upward. "I am going to check the generator. Stay in the loft until I tell you otherwise."

"We will," Emma said, her voice sounding steadier than she felt.

Coach stepped out of sight, her flashlight beam slicing briefly through the shadows before disappearing around the corner. The moment she was gone, the loft felt darker than ever.

The storm pounded the roof with a force that made the boards tremble. Snow slammed in waves against the windows. A roll of thunder cracked far across the valley. For a winter storm, it sounded almost like a summer one.

Zoey crawled closer to Emma. "Is the roof supposed to make that noise?"

"Yes," Riley said automatically, though her voice held a thin tremor. "Barns do that in big storms."

Harper hugged her blanket around her shoulders. "I do not like the dark."

Emma placed a hand on her arm. "It is okay. Coach is checking the generator. The lights will come back."

Another gust slammed into the barn, harder than before. A metal sign on the outer wall clanged loudly. A bucket in the aisle toppled with a hollow crash.

Ruby squealed in her stall.

Riley scrambled to the railing. "Ruby," she called softly. "Shhh. It is okay, girl."

Ruby tossed her head, her mane flipping wildly in the dim beam of a lantern someone must have stored below. She walked circles in her bedding, restless and confused.

Other horses reacted too. Fern pawed her stall. Daisy snorted and paced. Knightfall lifted his head sharply, ears turning in every direction, waiting for something familiar.

Emma swallowed hard. "We need to talk to them."

"We cannot go down," Zoey reminded her. "Coach said to stay up here."

"I know," Emma said, pressing her palm harder against the railing, "but they need to hear us."

Zoey nodded. "Then we talk."

The four girls leaned as close to the railing as they could without climbing over it.

"It is okay, Daisy," Zoey called softly. Her voice was warm, steady, full of affection. "You are safe. We are here."

Harper followed. "Fern, sweet girl, settle down. You are alright."

Riley whispered to Ruby again and again, her tone gentle. "You are okay. You are brave. Nothing can hurt you. We are right here."

Emma closed her eyes for a moment, gathering courage, before opening them again and speaking toward Knightfall's stall.

"Knightfall," she said softly. "It is just the storm. You have heard worse. I am here. Right above you."

He lifted his head toward the sound, ears pricked. His breath rumbled out in a deep sigh, calmer already.

For a few heartbeats, the barn steadied. The horses stopped turning circles. The stomping quieted. Even the storm seemed to pause, as if listening.

But the calm did not last long.

A high, thin whistle of wind pushed through the rafters. Snow blew in through a tiny gap near the roof. Somewhere in the back hallway, a door slammed shut. A loose rope knocked rhythmically against a metal ring.

Then they heard it.

A burst of loud popping sounds, electrical and sharp, like something sparking near the generator.

Emma jerked upright. "What was that?"

"Oh no," Zoey whispered. "That did not sound good."

Coach appeared again below them, flashlight still in hand. Her face was tight, her shoulders squared.

"Girls," she called, her voice firm and clear over the storm. "The generator will not stay on. I need you to stay calm and stay together. We will ride this out, but it might be a long night."

Harper whimpered softly.

Riley gripped the railing harder. "Do we have heat?"

"Battery heaters only," Coach said. "I am moving the portable ones into the center aisle. The horses will stay warm enough if they stay calm."

Emma felt that truth press against her chest. Calm was the key. But storms tested even the steadiest horse.

Below them, Coach moved swiftly, setting up battery lanterns that cast soft puddles of light around the aisle. The barn felt less suffocating in those small glows, but shadows still stretched long across the floor.

Zoey reached for her backpack and pulled out a hand sized camp lantern she had packed on a whim. "I brought this. Just in case."

Harper fumbled through her own bag and produced glow sticks. "I packed these too."

Riley's eyebrows rose. "Why do you have glow sticks?"

Harper shrugged. "Because I like being prepared. And also they look cool."

Zoey cracked one, shaking it until it glowed green. She set it along the loft railing. The soft color washed over their faces, giving the darkness a gentle hue.

Emma smiled faintly. "Good idea."

Another loud gust shook the barn. Snow dusted through the cracks above them. Somewhere near the tack room, something metal fell with a clatter that echoed down the aisle.

The horses stirred again.

Daisy swung her head. Fern whickered uneasily. Ruby pawed hard, tail swishing. Knightfall pinned his ears at the noise, though he did not move from his place.

Emma felt the instinct to go down and stand by his stall door. But Coach had given clear instructions. They needed to stay where they were for now.

Below, Coach checked the horses again, stopping at each stall to speak quietly to them. Her voice drifted up in gentle tones. The sound soothed the barn more effectively than any lantern or heater.

The girls watched, gripping the railing, their breath shallow in the cold air.

Another rumble of thunder rolled across the valley. It was faint, but enough to make a few horses flinch.

Riley whispered, "I hate storms."

Zoey nodded. "I do too."

Emma looked at both of them. "We can hate them together."

Harper added, "And survive them together."

There was something comforting in the way they said it all in one breath, as if their words created a small shield wrapping around them.

Time stretched. The storm continued. The wind raged against the barn. The lanterns flickered. The horses shuffled and snorted.

Then Coach called up to them again, more gently this time.

"Girls, listen. The worst of the storm will hit in the next few hours. I will need your help later, once things stabilize enough for you to come down. For now, stay warm, stay calm, and keep talking to the horses. They listen to your voices. It helps."

Emma nodded, though Coach could not see her.

"We will stay awake," Emma said aloud. "We will talk to them."

Coach gave a single nod and disappeared again into the hallway to check the outer doors.

The loft felt colder now, but also somehow safer. The glow sticks, lantern, fairy lights, and their blankets created a tiny pocket of light in the chaos.

The girls gathered their sleeping bags closer together, shoulder to shoulder, sitting facing the aisles so they could watch the horses.

They whispered to each other, their voices barely rising above the wind.

Zoey talked about Daisy's quirks. Riley shared the story of Ruby's first trail ride. Harper described Fern's favorite spots to be scratched. Emma talked softly about the way Knightfall trusted her even on days he was unsure.

As they spoke, the horses relaxed again. The storm still rattled the barn, but the steady hum of their shared voices filled the space with warmth.

Emma listened to the storm rage, listened to Knightfall breathing below, listened to her friends around her, and felt something strong and quiet settle in her chest.

They were in for a long night.

But they were together.

And that made all the difference.

Chapter Seven

The storm struck with renewed force just after midnight. The loft trembled as a blast of wind hammered the side of the barn, sending a plume of snow dust spiraling through the cracks in the rafters. Emma's eyes snapped open. She sat upright, heart thudding fast, blanket pooled at her waist. Around her, the other girls stirred in their sleeping bags, blinking into the semi-darkness.

"Is it morning?" Harper whispered, voice shaking.

"No," Zoey said softly. "The storm is just getting worse."

Riley rolled onto her side and stared over the railing toward the stalls below. "Ruby is moving again. I can hear her pacing."

Emma pressed her palm to the floorboards. She could feel Knightfall's weight shifting underneath her, the rhythmic scrape of hooves against bedding. Not frantic yet, but uneasy. Waiting. Listening.

She took a breath to steady herself. Storms had always unsettled her a little, but this one felt different, heavier and closer than any she remembered at Saddle Creek. The wind sounded alive, swirling and snarling against the walls.

A low groan echoed across the loft as another gust slammed the barn's outer siding. Zoey reached toward Emma and grabbed her hand without speaking. Emma squeezed back.

The battery lantern they had set near the railing cast a faint greenish glow from the glow sticks Harper had arranged around it. It was enough to see each other, but not enough to push back the shadows stretching across the rafters.

Below them, a horse whinnied sharply.

Emma froze. That had been Knightfall.

Then another sound split through the dark.

A loud snap.

Like canvas torn from its hooks.

The girls all jerked toward the aisle at once.

"What was that?" Zoey breathed.

Riley pushed herself up onto her knees, leaning over the railing. "It came from outside the back wall. That tarp near the door must have ripped."

Emma felt her skin prickle. A loose tarp could whip in the wind like a giant flag. Horses hated that sound. She had seen even calm lesson ponies lose their footing over a flapping piece of plastic in the past.

The snapping came again, louder this time.

SNAP. TWANG. WHIP.

The noise echoed through the rafters, sharp and unpredictable.

Knightfall rammed his shoulder into his stall wall with a thud. Fern pawed frantically at her door. Ruby's shrill squeal pierced the aisle as she struck sideways against her stall gate.

"Oh no," Harper whispered. "They are really scared."

Zoey crawled to the edge of the loft. "Coach?" she called, but her voice broke halfway through. "Coach, are you down there?"

No answer.

Emma felt panic flutter in her chest. Coach had been checking the generator earlier, and the back doors. She might be in the feed room or the equipment hallway. She might not have heard the tarp tearing.

Another blast of wind hit the barn and the tarp flapped violently. The sound cracked like a whip, long and painful. The horses reacted instantly.

Knightfall reared, hooves striking the air. His powerful body hit the stall wall, shaking the panels. Daisy backed into her water bucket, sending it crashing over. Ruby rammed her hip against her door with a loud clang.

Riley's voice rose, trembling but clear. "We cannot just sit here. They need us."

Zoey nodded, eyes wide with fear. "We have to go down."

But Emma remembered Coach's instructions clearly. *Do not come down unless I call for you.* The storm was dangerous. The horses were unpredictable. One wrong move could lead to someone getting kicked or knocked down.

"We cannot go near them if they are panicking," Emma said, voice firm even though her stomach twisted. "We need a plan."

"Plan, then help," Riley insisted. "But we cannot leave them like this. Ruby is going to hurt herself."

A loud crash from below made them all flinch. Something heavy had fallen. Another stall door rattled violently. Fern cried out in distress, a low, desperate sound.

Harper scrambled closer to the railing, her breath quick and uneven. "Emma, what do we do?"

Emma felt the pressure like a weight on her chest. She looked at her friends. She looked at the terrified shadows moving beneath them. She listened to the storm pounding the building. And she realized that this moment required her to be braver than she felt.

"We go down," Emma said quietly. "But carefully. And together."

Zoey swallowed hard. "You are sure?"

"Yes," Emma replied. "They know our voices. We will calm them with noise, not touch at first. We will not open a single stall door. We speak to them. We move slow. And we do not split up."

Riley nodded. "Okay. That works. We can do this."

Harper looked unsure, but she stood anyway. "I will stay behind you."

Emma reached for the lantern and switched it to its brightest setting. The warm beam flickered over their faces. She took one more breath, steady and long.

"Let us go," she said.

They climbed the ladder in a careful line, with Emma first, Zoey behind her, Riley next, and Harper last. When Emma reached the bottom, the cold hit her like a wall. The barn felt different in the dark, the air sharper and wilder. The storm outside roared, pressing in with a fury that made the wooden beams shiver.

The aisle was lit only by a half working battery lamp Coach had set on a bale of straw earlier. Its glow stretched weakly across the stalls, revealing the silhouettes of frightened horses.

Knightfall paced in a tight circle, breath quick, tail swishing. Ruby tossed her head with frantic energy. Fern struck her stall door repeatedly. Daisy stomped and blew loudly through her nose.

"They are terrified," Zoey whispered.

Emma held the lantern up high and forced her voice to stay steady. "Okay. Everyone to your horse. Not inside the stall. Stay just outside. Talk to them. Let them smell you. Let them hear you."

Zoey rushed to Daisy, stopping just shy of the door. "It is okay, girl. I am here. I am right here."

Daisy's ears flicked toward her, though the mare continued pacing.

Riley moved toward Ruby, planting her feet firmly. "Ruby, look at me. You know my voice. We have handled worse. You can settle."

Ruby snorted, then briefly touched her nose to the bars.

Harper approached Fern, her voice shaking but gentle. "Breathe, Fern. It is only the wind. You are safe."

Fern slowed her pawing for a heartbeat, listening.

Emma stood before Knightfall's stall. His eyes were wide, whites visible. His breath came in choppy bursts. His ears whipped back, then forward, then back again as the tarp snapped outside.

"Knightfall," Emma said softly, letting her voice fill the space between them. "You know me. I am right here. You have heard storms before. You are not alone."

He came toward her, halting only a step away. His nostrils flared as he caught her scent. Emma set her free hand quietly on the stall door, not reaching through yet.

Another crack of wind made the tarp outside snap like a whip again. Knightfall jerked back, nearly rearing again.

"We need to stop that tarp," Riley said through clenched teeth. "That is what is setting them off."

Zoey shook her head. "We cannot go outside. It is dangerous."

"Then we block the window closest to it," Emma said suddenly. "We cover it with something thick so they cannot see or hear it as much."

Riley blinked. "What can we use?"

Emma scanned the aisle, searching for anything heavy enough.

"Tarps," she said. "But smaller ones. And the big winter blankets. And maybe a spare stall mat if we can lift it."

Zoey followed her gaze. "We can stack the mats against the window panel. Make a buffer."

Harper's eyes widened. "But someone has to go near the window. Near the tarp outside. That is the loudest part."

Emma felt fear creep back into her stomach, cold and sharp.

But she also knew something else.

Knightfall needed her.

The barn needed her.

She could feel it deep in her bones.

"I will go," Emma said quietly.

Riley's head snapped up. "No. I should go. Ruby is calmer now. I can handle it."

Zoey stepped forward. "I will go with her."

Emma shook her head. "All of us will go. Together. We each hold one corner of the cover. We move slow. We keep our voices steady. And we stay close."

The horses reacted to her tone, ears flicking toward her, breaths settling just a touch.

Riley nodded. "We go as a team."

Zoey added, "We will calm them first, then act."

Harper grabbed the lantern. "Let us choose the thickest blankets."

They worked in a rush of careful movements. Riley hauled two winter turnout blankets from the storage rack. Zoey dragged one of the old stall mats toward the aisle. Harper grabbed extra hay bales to stack as bracing. Emma held the lantern and kept her voice low and soothing as she passed each stall.

When they were ready, the girls stood shoulder to shoulder facing the narrow side hallway that led to the window panel. The tarp outside cracked again, louder this time.

Zoey flinched. "That is awful."

Riley nodded. "Then let us stop the sound."

Emma took the first step down the hallway, lantern raised.

"I am right behind you," Zoey said.

"Me too," Riley added.

"Still here," Harper whispered, following with her glow stick.

The hallway was dim and cold, the air pushing in through tiny cracks. Snowflakes drifted along the edges of the floor. The window panel rattled violently as the wind hammered it from outside.

Emma swallowed. The panel shook again, threatening to pop inward.

Knightfall let out a sharp cry behind them.

"Do it now," Zoey said urgently. "Before they panic again."

Emma nodded and steadied herself.

This was it.

They had to quiet the storm inside the barn before the horses hurt themselves.

Together.

"On three," Emma whispered. "One. Two. Three."

They lifted the stall mat, pressed it against the shaking panel, and braced the blankets on top.

The tarp outside cracked again.

And the real trial began.

* * *

The stall mat hit the window panel with a heavy thump, muffling the roar of the tarp outside by only a fraction. The wind slammed into the outer wall again, rattling the frame and sending vibrations straight through Emma's arms. She pressed her shoulder harder against the mat, her breath sharp in her chest.

"Hold it steady," Riley said, lifting the far corner with both hands. "Do not let it slide."

"I am trying," Zoey grunted. She braced her knee against a hay bale, gripping another blanket to drape over the top. The hallway was narrow and cold. Snow snuck in through the gap along the edge of the window frame, melting instantly on Zoey's sleeve.

Harper stood behind them, holding the lantern high. "It keeps shifting! Should I get more hay bales?"

"Yes," Emma said quickly. "Build a brace on this side. Stack them tight."

Harper hurried away, her footsteps quick on the concrete.

The tarp outside cracked again, louder than before.

CRACK. WHIP. SNAP.

The sound tore through the hallway like a strike of lightning.

A split second later came another noise. One that made every hair rise along Emma's arms.

A sharp spiderweb of cracks appeared across the window panel.

Riley saw it first. "The glass is going."

"Keep the mat against it," Emma said, forcing her voice to stay steady. "We just need to hold until the wind slows."

Zoey blinked fast, eyes wide. "What if it shatters?"

55

"Then the mat will shield us," Emma said, though even saying it made her heart pound harder. Knightfall was somewhere behind her. The thought of flying shards reaching him or any of the horses made her sick.

Harper returned dragging another bale. "I brought more. Do I stack them on your left?"

"Against the bottom edge of the mat," Emma said. "It will stop it from sliding forward."

Harper shoved the first bale into position, then stacked the second one on top with shaking arms. The makeshift brace steadied the lower half of the mat.

The upper half was still exposed.

Riley took a deep breath and leaned her weight against it. "We need another blanket. Something heavy."

Zoey was already removing her spare winter pad from her backpack. "This one is thick."

As she handed it to Riley, another blast of wind hit the barn. The tarp outside ripped fully free of its corner hook with a horrible tearing sound. The loose end slapped the siding again and again like an enormous flag gone wild.

The horses reacted instantly.

Knightfall reared in his stall with a frightened scream. Ruby crashed into her door, hooves thudding. Daisy snorted violently and backed herself into the corner. Fern whinnied in a panic, stomping so hard the bedding flew.

Harper gasped. "This is getting worse. They are going to hurt themselves."

Emma squeezed her eyes shut for one heartbeat, then opened them again. Fear did not help. She had to think.

She had to lead.

She set her jaw. "We need to finish this wall. Then we go back to the stalls."

"We stabilize first, then calm them," Riley agreed. "If the window breaks, the sound will be ten times worse."

Zoey nodded, tears brimming from fear and cold. "Please let this work."

Together, they pressed the new blanket over the upper edge of the mat. The fabric slapped in the wind, trying to rip free. Emma leaned her shoulder in harder, feet slipping slightly in the snow collecting on the floor.

Riley braced from the right, her jaw clenched. "Push it in. Harder."

"I am trying," Zoey said, breath trembling.

Harper stacked another bale. "Almost done."

Emma felt the mat shift again. "Hold steady!"

The window shrieked as another gust hit it. The cracks spread in a jagged line across the glass.

"Please, please hold," Zoey whispered.

Then Emma saw it.

One small patch where the frame had pulled loose at the top. Snow whirled in through the gap. The wind whistled through it like a sharp flute, narrowing into a sound that felt made to panic horses.

"We need something to stop that gap," Emma said quickly. "Right there. Something you can wedge."

Riley scanned the hallway. "Tack trunk lid?"

"Too heavy," Zoey said.

Harper pointed behind her. "What about that old broom handle?"

Emma considered it. Thin, long, maybe just enough. "Yes. Grab it."

Harper darted to the corner, snatched the broom, and handed it over. Emma took one end and lifted it carefully.

"Zoey, lift the blanket," Emma said. "Riley, brace the mat."

They moved in a rhythm that had not existed before tonight, each girl instinctively adjusting to the other. Even Riley and Zoey moved in sync, no trace of the earlier fight in their motions.

Zoey lifted the blanket. Emma pushed the broom handle upward, sliding it into the narrow gap. The wood wedged into place, holding the frame tight.

The whistling stopped.

The wind rushed by outside, but the hallway grew quieter. More contained.

Emma exhaled in relief, her shoulders sagging for the first time in minutes.

"It worked," Harper said softly. "It really worked."

Riley leaned back against the doorframe, panting. "We are not done yet. We need to check the horses."

Emma grabbed the lantern. "Let us go."

They rushed back down the hallway, boots splashing through thin puddles of melted snow. The lantern beam swung wildly with their movements, illuminating the anxious shapes of the horses.

Knightfall's stall came first. He paced once, twice, then stopped when Emma's voice reached him.

"It is okay," Emma said gently. "We fixed the window. No more sound. I am here."

He turned sharply, stepped toward her, and pressed his muzzle against the bars. His breath washed warm over her fingers. Emma stroked his cheek without opening the door.

"That is it," she whispered. "Good boy. You are safe."

He sighed, nostrils softening.

Daisy was next. She stood in the corner, trembling slightly. Zoey stepped close.

"Daisy girl," she said softly. "Your brave heart is bigger than you think."

Daisy stretched her neck and touched Zoey's sleeve. Zoey's relief showed in her whole posture.

Fern had calmed only a little. She stomped the floor once, but Harper spoke to her in a steady hum. "I am here. I am right here." Fern lowered her head and pressed it against the door.

Finally, they approached Ruby.

Ruby tossed her head once more, but it was not the wild panic from earlier. Her eyes still showed fear, but her ears flicked toward Riley.

Riley planted both feet, shoulders square. "Ruby," she said quietly. "Listen to me. You are the strongest horse I know. You have handled trailer rides and creek crossings and shows where ponies tried to eat your tail. You can handle this too."

Ruby blew a warm breath into Riley's hands.

Zoey stepped forward hesitantly. "You want help?"

Riley looked at her for a long moment. Neither spoke. Then Riley nodded once. "Yes."

Zoey came beside her, both girls standing shoulder to shoulder before Ruby's stall. Ruby sniffed Zoey's hand cautiously, then returned her attention to Riley.

"You two are good together," Zoey said softly. "And so is she."

Riley swallowed. "Thanks."

A small thaw. A small peace.

Emma felt warmth spread in her chest. Under the pressure of the storm, something had finally begun to heal.

But the night was far from over.

Another gust shook the barn, though quieter than before. The blankets and mat muffled most of the noise, but not all. The storm still howled outside, pushing against the outer walls.

Zoey looked around. "Do you think Coach is okay?"

"We should check on her," Riley said.

Emma nodded. "One person only. The rest stay here with the horses."

"I will go," Riley said. "Ruby trusts you more right now, Emma. Stay with her."

"But you should not go alone," Zoey said instantly. "I will go with you."

Harper raised a hand. "I will stay with Emma."

Emma nodded. "Good. We need to keep the horses calm."

Riley and Zoey set off down the center aisle. The lantern cast long shadows against the walls as they disappeared into the dim hallway where the feed room stood.

Emma and Harper stayed near the stalls, whispering to the horses, keeping their tones soft and steady.

Minutes stretched thin. The storm whipped at the barn, but the window held. Knightfall stayed near Emma, calm now but watchful. Ruby shifted closer to her stall door as if sensing the girls' quiet determination.

Then footsteps returned.

Riley's and Zoey's faces appeared in the lantern glow.

"We found her," Riley said, breathless. "She is okay."

Zoey nodded. "The generator room door jammed shut. She was trying to pry it open from the inside. We told her the window is patched."

Emma exhaled a long breath she did not realize she had been holding. "Thank goodness."

"She is coming," Zoey said. "She just needed a moment to check the outer latch."

Coach appeared shortly after, dusted with snow, hair windblown, flashlight in hand.

"You girls did well," Coach said firmly. "The window would have blown in without that support. I saw your brace. That took brains and courage."

Zoey beamed despite her exhaustion. Riley ducked her head. Harper blushed. Emma smiled softly.

Coach walked to Knightfall's stall first, checking his breathing, then moved down the row of horses. When she reached Ruby, she paused and looked at Riley and Zoey together.

"You two did that as a team," Coach said.

Riley nodded. "We had to."

Zoey gave a shy smile. "We wanted to."

Coach nodded with approval. "Good."

The storm continued to howl, but it no longer pierced the barn the way it had. The window brace held. The horses breathed easier. The girls leaned on each other. The worst of the fear had passed.

Emma looked around the barn, lantern light flickering across her friends' tired faces, the horses settling into quieter rhythms.

They had not slept.

They were cold.

They were exhausted.

But they had done something brave. Something important. Together.

Coach motioned to the loft ladder. "Go up and rest for a bit. I will watch the horses."

Emma hesitated. "We can stay—"

"Rest," Coach said gently. "You will need your strength. The storm is not over yet."

The girls exchanged glances. Riley nodded first. "Okay."

Zoey followed. Harper went next.

Emma paused, her eyes drifting to Knightfall. "Good night, boy. You did so well."

He touched her sleeve before stepping back into his hay.

Emma climbed the ladder last. When she reached the top, the loft felt warmer than before. Softer. She sank into her sleeping bag, muscles trembling with relief.

Below, the barn creaked and groaned, but the horses stayed calm. Emma heard Coach's footsteps passing quietly from stall to stall.

The storm would rage for hours still.

But they had already faced its worst moment and held strong.

In the quiet glow of their lanterns, surrounded by friends and the steady comfort of horses, Emma felt something she had not felt all night.

Hope.

Chapter Eight

The storm dragged on through the early hours, never settling into a rhythm gentle enough to ignore. The barn seemed to breathe with each gust, its beams creaking softly under the pressure. Emma rested in her sleeping bag with her head propped against her folded jacket. Every noise reached her. Every shift of the horses below kept her half awake.

She had drifted into a light doze when a new sound pulled her upright.

A hollow thump. Then another. And a low groan.

At first she thought the wind had knocked something loose outside again. But then the thumping came a third time, slower, heavier. It did not match the pattern of a rattling door or a slamming branch.

It sounded like a horse striking the floor with its hooves.

Emma blinked rapidly, trying to clear her vision. A faint blush of pale gray light peeked through the loft window, suggesting dawn was trying to push through the storm. The lantern beside her had dimmed to a soft glow.

She pushed her blanket off and sat up fully.

Riley stirred beside her. "What time is it?"

"Still early," Emma murmured. "But something is wrong."

Zoey sat up as well, her curls flattened on one side. "Wrong how?"

"That sound," Emma said. "It is coming from Fern's stall."

Harper moaned sleepily. "Fern is fine. She was fine earlier."

Another thump echoed through the barn.

Harper sat bolt upright now, eyes wide.

"I am checking," Emma said. She grabbed the lantern and crawled toward the loft ladder. Her legs felt stiff from the cold and from the hours of tension earlier, but her determination was steady.

The others followed, the four of them moving together like they always did when the barn needed them.

They descended the ladder carefully, even though their hearts told them to rush.

The aisle smelled strongly of hay and cold metal. The storm still howled outside, though the worst of the wind seemed to have eased slightly. Battery lanterns Coach had hung earlier lit the aisle in warm puddles of gold.

Emma walked quickly toward Fern's stall.

Harper reached it first.

"Fern?" Harper whispered, kneeling by the bars. "What are you doing, sweet girl?"

Fern stood with her belly tucked up, sweat foaming along her flanks despite the cold. Her head hung low, and she pawed at the floor once more before lifting her hind leg and drawing it tight to her belly.

Harper gasped. "No. No, no, no."

Zoey placed a gentle hand on Harper's shoulder. "She looks uncomfortable."

Riley swallowed, stepping close. "She looks like she is colicking."

Emma's stomach twisted. She had seen colic only once before, with an older lesson horse the previous summer. That horse had pawed the ground, rolled, and refused to eat his hay. It had taken the vet hours to stabilize him. Colic was serious. It was dangerous. It did not wait for daylight or ask permission.

Harper's hands shook as she touched Fern's cheek through the bars. "Please do not be sick. Please."

Fern groaned again, shifting weight. She tried to stretch out as if to lie down.

Emma stepped forward. "We need Coach."

Coach had been awake most of the night, checking the barn every hour. She had gone to reset a failing lantern near the hay room not long before the girls woke. Emma turned and ran toward the far aisle, her boots slapping the concrete. She rounded the corner and almost collided with Coach, who was already striding toward them.

"I heard something," Coach said, her voice steady but alert. "What is going on?"

"It is Fern," Emma said. "She is showing signs of colic."

Coach quickened her pace and reached the stall quickly, kneeling beside Harper. "Tell me everything that happened."

Harper's voice broke. "She started pawing. And groaning. She looks at her belly. She seems... she seems in pain."

Coach reached through the bars and touched Fern's neck. "Her skin is damp. And she is breathing harder than she should." She pressed her ear to Fern's side for a full minute while the girls held their breath.

Coach stood again, face tight. "Her gut sounds are quiet."

Zoey bit her lip. "Is it bad?"

Coach nodded once. "It is concerning. We need to walk her. We need to keep her up and moving so she does not roll."

Harper's eyes filled instantly. "I can walk her. I can do it."

Coach put a gentle hand on her shoulder. "Not alone. She may try to drop. You need backup."

"I will help," Emma said immediately.

"So will I," Zoey said.

Riley added, "Me too."

Harper wiped her face with her sleeve. "Thank you."

Coach unlatched the stall with careful movements. She opened the door slowly, giving Fern space. The mare hesitated, shifting weight uncertainly, then stepped out with a tired groan.

Emma had never seen Fern look so small. Usually she carried herself like a queen, soft hooves lifting with elegant steps. Now she looked fragile, trembling, her coat damp despite the chill.

Once Fern was out, Coach handed the lead rope to Harper. "Walk her slowly up and down the aisle. Keep her head up if she tries to roll. Talk to her. Let her hear your voice."

Harper nodded, swallowing fear. She placed a gentle hand on Fern's neck. "We got you," she whispered. "We will help you."

Fern leaned into her touch for a moment before taking a few tentative steps.

Coach turned to the other girls. "Emma on Harper's right. Zoey on her left. Riley behind them in case Fern backs up."

Riley nodded firmly. "Got it."

"And stay calm," Coach said. "Horses feel everything. If you wobble, she wobbles harder."

The girls fell into place immediately.

Harper led Fern slowly down the aisle. Fern's hooves clicked softly on the concrete. She paused every few steps, lifting her hind leg again as if trying to stretch away the pain.

"It is okay," Harper whispered. "I am right here. Keep walking. Good girl."

Zoey walked close enough to offer support but not crowd. "You are doing great, Harper."

Emma kept an eye on Fern's breathing. It was still too fast. The mare's sides heaved slightly with every breath. Sweat clung to her winter coat, making her look soaked in some places.

They made one slow pass up the aisle, then another. Outside, the storm continued to rage, but inside the barn everything narrowed to the small rhythmic shuffle of Fern's steps.

Knightfall watched them with alert eyes, ears pricked toward Emma. Ruby snorted, unsettled. Daisy paced once, then leaned her head over her door, as if understanding something was wrong.

After the third pass, Fern stumbled.

Harper gasped and tightened her hold.

Emma reacted quickly. "Support her on the left. Keep her walking."

Zoey guided Fern gently while Harper steadied her on the right. Riley stepped in quickly on the back side to keep the mare from swinging too far.

"Good job," Coach called from the tack room doorway. "Stay patient. You are doing well."

Emma took slow breaths. She forced the fear back. Panic did not belong here.

After another twenty minutes of steady walking, Fern's breathing eased slightly. She lifted her head a little higher, though sweat still darkened her coat.

Harper looked toward Coach. "Is she getting better?"

Coach hesitated before answering. "She is not worsening, which is good. But she is not improving fast enough. We need to call the vet."

Harper's face paled. "But the roads..."

"The vet can get here if needed," Coach said. "The problem is calling him. The landline is out. We have to try the emergency signal box near the office."

Riley frowned. "Does it work during power outages?"

"It is supposed to," Coach said. "But storms like this sometimes knock the tower."

Zoey put a hand to her chest. "What do we do if it does not work?"

Coach looked toward Fern, her brow furrowed. "We improvise. But first we try."

"I can go," Riley said quickly.

"You are staying with Fern," Coach replied. "Emma, Zoey, Harper stay too."

Coach turned to Emma. "I need your calm. And your voice."

Emma's stomach tightened, but she nodded. "I will keep her walking."

Coach looked at Harper last. "You are doing something brave, Harper. Stay strong."

Harper bit her lip and nodded, fighting tears.

Coach headed toward the office, her flashlight beam bouncing along the wall.

Fern's legs trembled again. Harper kept her walking, though she could barely keep her hands from shaking.

Emma walked close to Fern's right shoulder. "You are doing so well," she whispered. "Just a bit longer."

Zoey added gently, "Good girl, Fern. Keep moving."

Riley walked backward ahead of them, making sure Fern did not surge or drift. "We have you," Riley murmured. "I know it hurts. But you can get through it."

They made two more passes up the aisle. Fern stumbled once more, but Harper steadied her with a soft touch.

Emma could feel the fear rising again. Fern looked weaker with each minute. Sweat soaked her chest now. Her tail hung limp.

"Harper," Emma said quietly, "talk to her. Tell her something from home."

Harper swallowed hard. "Okay." She leaned close. "Remember the summer pasture? The one with the clover? You love it there. And the fallen log you always sniff. And the apple tree at the far end. I promise you can go back there. Just keep walking."

Fern seemed to lean into her words, taking slow steps that shimmered with effort.

Coach appeared again from the hallway. Her expression told Emma everything before she spoke.

"The emergency line is down," Coach said.

Harper's breath caught. "No."

Zoey closed her eyes. Riley cursed under her breath.

Emma tightened her hand on the lead rope. "Then what do we do?"

Coach straightened, her voice strong even through the worry. "We do everything we can. We keep her moving. We watch for signs of worsening. And when the wind slows enough, I will go to the road with a signal flare to flag down help."

Harper nodded, trembling but determined. "Okay. We keep her walking."

They continued pacing up and down the aisle. Over and over. Step by step.

Minutes turned into nearly an hour.

Fern stumbled again, but this time did not fall. Her breathing steadied, though her sides still twitched weakly.

Zoey kept her voice steady. "She needs encouragement. Keep talking."

Harper sniffed and wiped her face. "You are the bravest horse I know. I love you so much."

Fern flicked her ears backward, catching the sound.

Riley moved closer. "She is listening. She wants to keep going."

Emma noticed something then. Fern's breathing seemed different. Not easier, exactly. But more steady. More rhythmic.

"Coach," Emma said quietly. "She is leveling out."

Coach approached and placed her hands gently along Fern's belly, listening. She pressed her ear against Fern's side again and waited.

After a long moment, Coach exhaled. Relief softened her shoulders. "Her gut is making noise again. That is a good sign."

Harper sagged against Fern, whispering thank you over and over.

Zoey wiped her eyes. Riley turned away for a moment to regain herself.

Emma let out a breath that felt like it had been locked inside her since the moment Fern first pawed the ground.

"Do we keep walking?" Emma asked.

Coach nodded. "Yes. Slow walking for another twenty minutes. Then she can rest. But she has turned a corner." She looked at Harper with a small, warm smile. "You helped her through it."

Harper covered her face with one hand, overwhelmed. "I was so scared."

Coach touched her shoulder. "Caring for a sick horse is one of the hardest things you can do. And you did it while a storm tried to tear down the roof. That is courage."

Harper nodded, tears streaming freely now.

Zoey hugged her. Riley joined after a moment. Emma wrapped her arms around all three. For a moment they stood together, a tight circle in the barn aisle, while Fern breathed slowly beside them.

The storm groaned outside, but the barn felt different now. Stronger. Warmer.

They finished the final laps, then helped Fern settle back into her stall with fresh bedding and a bucket of warm water. Harper stayed at her door, stroking her cheek until Fern's breathing slowed into a soft rhythm of exhaustion.

Coach checked her again and finally stepped back with relief. "She will need monitoring, but I think she will be alright."

Harper covered her mouth with both hands, laugh-crying. "Thank you."

Coach nodded. "You all did this. You did not give up on her."

Emma looked at her friends, at the horses, at the barn lit softly by lanterns. Her chest felt full in the best way.

They had faced fear.

They had worked together.

And they had saved a life.

The storm still blew, but it did not feel quite so frightening anymore.

Inside Saddle Creek, there was light.

There was warmth.

There were horses breathing quietly again.

And there were friends holding each other up.

Emma breathed the warm barn air and felt the truth of it settle deep.

They were going to make it through this night.

Together.

Chapter Nine

The storm had begun to lose its sharp edge, but the barn still shook with every gust. Dawn had not yet arrived. The world outside remained black and fierce, but inside Saddle Creek, a different kind of storm settled.

Emma knelt beside Harper outside Fern's stall. Fern's breathing had steadied, but her sides still rose and fell with effort. Steam drifted from her coat. Harper stroked her muzzle with trembling fingers.

"We are not done yet," Emma whispered gently. "She is better, but we need to keep her warm."

Harper nodded, though her hands shook. "I will stay right here. She needs me."

"You will not be alone," Emma said, and meant it with her whole heart.

Down the aisle, Coach slammed the generator room door shut. "Still nothing," she muttered. "This storm has taken out more lines than I thought."

Zoey appeared beside her, holding a clipboard she must have grabbed from the office. "Coach, we need a plan. A list of priorities."

Coach looked surprised. "A list?"

Zoey nodded firmly, determination lighting her face. "Logistics are my thing. Tell me what we must do and I will organise it."

Coach hesitated for only a moment. Then she handed Zoey her flashlight. "Check the heat lamps first. Then make sure the battery lanterns will last until morning."

Zoey nodded and hurried off, flipping to a blank page and writing as she walked.

Riley moved between the stalls with quiet purpose. Ruby nickered to her as she passed. Knightfall pressed his nose over his door. Daisy swished her tail but kept still.

"Listen up, everyone," Riley said softly to the row of horses. "Nothing else is falling. No more tarp noises. You are safe. I promise."

Her voice surprised Emma. It carried authority and calm, like someone who knew exactly what fear felt like and refused to let it win.

Even Coach turned, eyebrows raised slightly.

Riley continued speaking to each horse as she moved along the aisle. Her voice wove through the darkness, steadying the animals better than any equipment.

"You are not alone," she whispered to Daisy.

"We are here," she murmured to Knightfall.

"You are brave," she told Ruby, her hand against the mare's cheek.

"Good horses. All of you are good."

Their bodies relaxed visibly. Emma felt something warm and powerful settle inside her chest.

Riley was not fearless. She just chose to be brave for them.

The barn lights flickered once as a gust rattled the siding. Harper jumped, but Emma steadied her.

"It is okay," Emma said softly. "We have done the hardest part. We will take the rest minute by minute."

"Will the vet come?" Harper whispered.

Emma hesitated, then nodded. "Coach will find a way."

As if summoned by that faith, Coach returned at that exact moment, snow on her shoulders and a flare tube under one arm.

"The wind dropped enough for me to try the road," Coach said. "I sent up a flare. The vet saw it from a distance. He is coming now."

Harper covered her face, shoulders shaking with relief. Fern flicked an ear as if sensing the shift.

"We keep her walking until he arrives," Coach said. "Slow pace. No stopping unless she needs a drink."

"I can do it," Harper whispered.

Emma stood. "I will walk with you."

Zoey reappeared, breathless, clipboard full. "Heat lamps good. Lanterns good. I also stacked hay near the warmest side in case a horse needs more bedding."

Coach nodded with real admiration. "Great work, Zoey."

Zoey flushed with pride.

Riley approached next. "All horses are calmer. Ruby even yawned."

"Keep doing what you are doing," Coach said softly. "You are steadying the whole barn."

Riley looked away quickly, but Emma saw the small smile she tried to hide.

Together, the girls resumed walking Fern. This time, Fern moved more willingly, leaning into Harper's voice every time she faltered.

Emma walked on the right side, matching Fern's steps. Riley walked at her flank, making sure she did not swing too wide. Zoey followed behind with a blanket, ready to drape it if Fern shivered.

Every few minutes Coach checked Fern's belly with practiced hands. Each time she nodded more confidently.

"She is fighting," Coach said quietly. "She wants to push through this."

"So will we," Harper murmured.

Outside, a distant engine broke through the wind.

Riley straightened. "The vet."

Coach jogged to the front doors, pushed them open, and waved her flashlight twice. Snow blew in around her boots as a truck fought its way into the yard. Headlights sliced through the dark like a promise.

Relief swept through the barn in a silent wave.

The vet hurried inside, stamping snow from his coat. "Rough night," he said, already unzipping his bag. "Where is the patient?"

"Fern," Harper whispered. "Please help her."

The vet approached the mare with calm, practiced movements. He checked her pulse, her hydration, her belly sounds. Fern leaned into him, exhausted but more responsive.

"She did good," the vet said. "You all did. She is stable enough for medication now."

Harper let out a sound between a sob and a laugh.

The vet administered the medicine, rubbed Fern's neck gently, and stepped back.

"She will need quiet and monitoring," he said. "But she is turning the corner."

Harper hugged Emma without warning. Emma hugged her back just as tightly.

Zoey threw her arms around both of them. Riley joined a second later, pulling the circle even tighter.

Four girls.

One storm.

One horse who had fought through the night.

And a friendship that felt stronger than it ever had before.

When the vet left and the doors closed again, dawn finally began to lighten the barn. The horses breathed softly. The lanterns glowed warm. The storm's edge faded into a tired, pale sky.

Fern shifted in her stall, lowering her head to her hay in a small, tentative nibble.

Harper cried again, but this time the tears were full of joy.

"She is eating," Zoey whispered.

"That is a good sign," Riley said, smiling for real.

Emma reached out and held Harper's hand. "She is going to be okay."

Coach stood behind them, arms folded, eyes full of pride. "You girls saved her. You used your heads and your hearts. You worked like a real team."

Outside, snow continued to drift, but without fury now. The barn glowed in the rising light, warmth returning to every corner.

It had been the hardest night they had ever faced.

But they had not faced it alone.

And by early morning, as Fern rested comfortably and the storm softened at last, something deep and unbreakable had settled between the girls.

They had saved a horse.

They had saved each other.

And Saddle Creek felt like home more than ever.

Chapter Ten

Morning arrived slowly, hesitating as if unsure the storm had truly spent its strength. Pale gold light crept across Saddle Creek, settling gently over the drifts piled high around the barns. The wind had eased into tired sighs. The sky, washed clean of its fury, stretched clear and soft, streaked with early pink.

Emma stepped out of the front barn door and drew a deep breath of crisp air. The storm had left behind a world transformed. Snow lay knee deep in the yard, smooth and untouched except for the path carved earlier by the vet's truck. Even that had been half buried again by drifting flakes.

The vet had stayed through the last hours of the night to make sure Fern remained stable. Now his truck stood near the gate, heat still rising from its hood. He walked the final stretch of the access road and shook his head.

"I cannot get through without help," he said. "The snowplough has not reached this far yet."

Coach joined him, hands on her hips, taking stock of the blocked road. "Then we make a path."

Zoey emerged from the barn behind them, hair pulled into a messy bun, cheeks pink from warmth and exhaustion. "We can shovel," she said. "All of us."

Riley followed with a snow shovel in each hand. "Already ahead of you."

Harper appeared last, her tired eyes brightening when she saw the sunlight. "Fern is eating again," she said softly. "The vet says she is doing well."

Emma hugged her. "Good."

Coach clapped her hands lightly. "Grab tools. Shovels, brooms, anything you can find. We start with a narrow path wide enough for the truck to move."

The girls scattered, gathering every workable tool they could find. Emma took a shovel. Zoey brought two stable brooms. Harper carried a pitchfork, which Coach approved for breaking the ice layer. Riley hauled another shovel from the maintenance shed.

They lined up at the edge of the drifted road.

"Slow and steady," Coach said. "Lift from your legs, not your backs."

Emma dug the first scoop, the cold stinging her gloves. The snow was soft on top but packed hard beneath. Riley broke a path with powerful motions, using a rhythm that made her look like she was working out her frustrations. Zoey brushed the cleared line smooth behind them, creating a corridor. Harper attacked the icy bits with sharp thrusts of her pitchfork. Coach worked at the far end, pulling snow away from the gate.

The sky brightened. A few birds even called from the trees, as if relieved to hear themselves again.

Minutes passed. Then more. Then more still.

Eventually, Emma paused to catch her breath. Riley stopped too, leaning on her shovel.

Zoey glanced between them. "You two need a break?"

Riley shook her head. "Actually... Zoey, can we talk? Just for a second."

Zoey froze. "Now?"

"Yes," Riley said quietly. "Now."

Emma gave Harper a gentle nudge. "Let them talk. We will go help Coach for a bit."

The two of them walked a little farther down the path. Emma kept one eye on Fern's stall window, but the mare's silhouette seemed peaceful.

Zoey and Riley stood facing each other, boots half buried in snow.

Riley spoke first. Her voice was small, but honest. "I was unfair to you. For weeks."

Zoey hesitated. "Riley..."

"No," Riley said. "I need to say this. I felt overshadowed. Like you were becoming better at everything without trying. And instead of working harder, I pushed you away."

Zoey inhaled slowly. "I did not know you felt like that."

"I know," Riley said, rubbing her glove over her forehead. "I did not explain. I just snapped. Again and again. And you did not deserve it."

Zoey's eyes softened. "I never wanted to compete with you. I just wanted us to be friends."

Riley nodded slowly. "I do too. I miss how we were before. And tonight... working together... it reminded me that we are better as a team."

Zoey took one step closer. "We can start again."

A smile tugged at Riley's lips. "Really?"

"Really," Zoey said. "But next time you feel overshadowed, you tell me instead of exploding like a volcano."

Riley laughed, a tired but real sound. "Deal."

They hugged awkwardly at first, then tightly, holding on with the relief of two people who had worried they lost something important.

Emma smiled from a distance. Harper smiled too. Last night had shaken them, exhausted them, scared them, but it had also mended something that had been cracking for months.

Zoey and Riley rejoined the group. No one teased. No one pointed it out. Everyone simply felt the change, warm and real.

"Let us get this finished," Riley said, lifting her shovel with new energy.

They worked harder after that, passing tools back and forth, helping each other lift heavy drifts, laughing when Riley tripped into a mound up to her waist, cheering when Zoey cleared a perfect stretch of the icy ground.

Midway through clearing the outer stretch of road, Emma stopped suddenly.

"What is that?" she asked, pointing toward the property line beyond the fence.

Zoey pushed her curls back. "Tracks."

Harper squinted. "Those are hoofprints."

Riley walked closer. "But not from our horses. The shoes look different."

Coach approached, brushing snow from her gloves. She studied the tracks carefully. "Those belong to a roaming ranch horse in the valley. He wanders during storms. Comes down from the forestry ridge every summer."

Emma's brows lifted. "Does he belong to someone?"

"Yes," Coach said. "Old ranch family down on the south road. He has a habit of slipping through their back gate. Shows up in odd places. Sometimes following trails. Sometimes causing mischief."

Zoey smiled. "An adventurer."

Riley tilted her head. "Is he safe?"

"He is clever," Coach said. "But unpredictable. And sometimes he looks for other horses when he gets lonely."

Emma looked at the prints leading toward the tree line. "Will he come back?"

"Perhaps," Coach said. "Most likely in summer. Horses like him prefer warm weather for wandering."

Riley shivered. "Let us hope he does not wander near the back trails when we ride."

Coach laughed softly. "If he does, you will know. And then you will have a story you will never forget."

Emma's heart gave a small excited flutter.

A wandering horse.

A mystery.

A summer trail.

Something new waiting on the horizon.

She tucked the thought away. A seed for later. A hint of the adventures still ahead.

The girls finished clearing the path just as the sun lifted above the snowy ridge. Light spilled across the barn, turning the snow into sparkling crystals. The vet drove out with a thankful wave, tires crunching safely through the road they created.

Harper ran to Fern's stall one more time. The mare lifted her head and nickered softly. Harper pressed her forehead to Fern's. "Thank you," she whispered.

Emma felt a deep satisfaction, the quiet kind that came after struggle. The barn had survived the night. The horses were safe. Friendships had healed. And the storm had left behind new possibilities hidden in the snow.

Coach gathered them in the yard. "You girls should be proud. Not many riders your age could do what you did here. Saddle Creek is lucky to have you."

Zoey beamed. Riley grinned. Harper hugged her coat around herself as if holding her relief close.

And Emma felt it too.

A sense of belonging that ran deeper than anything she could explain.

She looked toward the tree line where the mysterious hoofprints disappeared.

Summer was far away, but a small part of her already wondered what stories waited when the snow melted.

Chapter Eleven

The first true light of morning touched Saddle Creek like a healing hand. After the long and frightening night, the barn basked in a soft, golden glow that seemed to slow time itself. Snow blanketed every roofline and fence rail, smoothing sharp edges into gentle curves. Icicles glittered along the gutters. Mist rose faintly from the paddock as the sun warmed the snow.

Inside, the barn exhaled in a long, quiet sigh. Horses shifted lazily, the panic of the storm behind them now. A few flicked their tails. One or two dozed. The whole place felt wrapped in a peaceful, sleepy hush.

Emma walked down the aisle with a heavy blanket draped over her shoulders. Her legs ached, her eyes stung from lack of sleep, and her throat felt scratchy from talking all night to keep Knightfall calm. But for the first time since yesterday morning, she felt steady inside.

She stopped at Knightfall's stall and rested her forehead gently against the door. He stepped forward immediately and breathed onto her cheeks, warm and soft.

"Good morning," Emma whispered. "We made it."

Knightfall nosed her coat pocket, searching for the treat she had not brought yet. Emma laughed under her breath.

"Okay. Let me get something for you."

She found the treat bin left on the feed cart. She took two, then reconsidered and took only one. "You deserve ten," she told him, "but Coach will give me the look if I spoil you right after a storm."

She fed him the treat and ran her hand along his cheek. His coat had dried, but he still smelled faintly of the sweat and fear from the worst hours of the night. Emma stroked him gently until she felt his body loosen.

"You were brave," she whispered.

Knightfall blinked slowly, as if he understood.

She stayed with him for several quiet minutes. It felt good to just breathe. To be still. To let the fear drain out of her body and disappear into the morning air.

After a while, Zoey appeared at the far end of the aisle, wrapped in her purple winter coat with her curls tumbling around her face. She yawned so widely that her eyes watered. Still, her smile was warm.

"Emma," Zoey said softly. "You okay?"

Emma nodded. "Mostly. You?"

Zoey lowered her voice. "Better now."

They met near Daisy's stall, exchanging the kind of half hug that comes when both people are exhausted but relieved to see each other safe.

Daisy stretched her neck over the door and puffed warm air at Zoey's cheek. Zoey touched the mare's muzzle lightly. "She settled around five," she said. "Slept for a full hour. She looks so peaceful now."

Emma smiled. "We all look better now."

Zoey took a long breath, letting it fill her chest fully. "I feel like I aged five years in one night."

Emma nodded. "Me too. Maybe more."

They both laughed quietly. It felt good.

At the far end of the aisle, Coach finished checking a water bucket. She straightened with a small groan, pressing her hand to her lower back.

Emma called softly, "Coach? Are you alright?"

Coach waved off the concern with a tired smile. "Old bones. Long night. I am fine."

Zoey stepped closer. "Do you want help with morning checks?"

"No," Coach said. "I want you girls to breathe. We will handle chores slowly today. You have earned some rest."

Emma and Zoey exchanged glances. Coach did not say things like that lightly.

Harper emerged next from the tack room, carrying a folded blanket. She looked tiny inside her oversized jacket, eyes puffy, but she moved with a sense of purpose.

Emma walked toward her. "How is Fern?"

Harper's expression softened in a way that made Emma's heart lift. "Eating. Drinking. Resting. The vet said he will stop by again later."

Emma hugged her tightly. Harper clung back with relief.

"You were amazing last night," Emma whispered. "You kept her walking even when you were scared."

Harper swallowed. "She needed me."

"And you were there," Emma said. "That is what matters."

When they pulled apart, Harper wiped her eyes quickly and forced a small smile.

Riley wandered down the aisle a few moments later, rubbing her eyes with her glove. Ruby followed her movements with calm interest, ears pricked. Riley still looked tired, but there was something different in her face this morning. Softer. Lighter.

"Morning," Riley said quietly.

Zoey gave her a gentle nudge. "Hey."

Riley smiled back, a real one. "Hey."

Emma felt something settle between them. A steadiness. A new start.

Coach clapped her hands lightly to gather them. Her voice was soft but clear. "Girls, come here for a moment."

They gathered near the middle of the aisle. The horses watched, ears flicking, as if sensing that something important was about to be said.

Coach folded her arms loosely. "Last night tested everyone here. Horses and humans. You worked together. You stayed calm under pressure. You listened. You trusted each other. And because of that, the barn is safe and Fern is recovering."

Her eyes softened as she looked at Harper. "You did everything right. You protected your horse."

Harper's eyes filled. "Thank you."

Coach turned to Emma. "You led when leadership was needed."

Emma felt her cheeks warm. "I just did what I could."

"That is what leadership is," Coach said gently. "Doing what you can when it matters."

Then Coach looked at Zoey and Riley together. "And the two of you stepped up in a way that changed this night. You steadied the barn. You steadied each other."

Zoey and Riley exchanged warm smiles that held the weight of weeks of confusion now lifted.

Coach drew a slow breath. "Saddle Creek is proud of you. I am proud of you."

Emma felt the words settle inside her like sunlight.

Coach then softened her voice. "For now, slow chores, warm drinks, and quiet time with your horses. We will take the day in small steps."

She walked away to check Knightfall's hay, leaving the girls in the quiet of the aisle.

Riley nudged Zoey. "Coffee?"

Zoey snorted. "Hot chocolate, actually."

Riley grinned. "Fine. Hot chocolate."

Emma smiled at both of them. "I will help Harper with Fern first."

Harper shook her head. "She is okay. Go drink something warm."

But Emma saw the tired lines around Harper's eyes and shook her head. "I will stay with you anyway."

Harper nodded gratefully.

Zoey and Riley wandered toward the lounge while Emma and Harper returned to Fern's stall. The mare lifted her head and nosed Harper's sleeve gently. Her eyes were much clearer now, though she still moved slowly.

Harper opened the door just enough to slip inside. She leaned against Fern's shoulder carefully and exhaled as if letting go of the last of her fear.

Emma stood outside, watching quietly.

After a few minutes, Harper said softly, "Do you ever get scared you will not be enough for your horse?"

Emma leaned against the stall door. "Sometimes. More than I admit. But what happened last night showed you are enough. More than enough."

Harper gave a tiny smile. "Fern trusts me."

"And that trust is earned," Emma said. "You earned it."

Harper stroked Fern's neck gently. "I could not have done it without all of you."

Emma nodded. "We all needed each other."

More quiet passed between them, the kind that felt soft and healing.

After a while, Harper stepped back out and closed the stall gently.

"You should drink something warm too," she told Emma.

"Only if you come with me," Emma said.

Harper nodded.

They joined the others in the lounge, where Coach had left a pot of steaming hot chocolate on the counter. The mugs were mismatched. The heat fogged the little window. The room smelled like cinnamon and respite.

Riley sat on one of the couches with a thick blanket around her shoulders. Zoey sat beside her, the two of them sharing a tired but genuine laugh about Riley's dramatic fall into a snow drift earlier during the shoveling.

Emma and Harper sank into the couch across from them. Coach sat in the corner chair, sipping her tea, watching them like a shepherd who had finally seen her flock settle.

Riley glanced at Zoey. "You know... I meant what I said outside earlier. I want things to be good again."

Zoey nodded. "They are starting to be."

Riley stared into her mug. "I felt like everyone outgrew me."

Zoey's voice softened. "We never did."

Riley looked up. "I thought you did. That is why I acted out. It was stupid."

"It was human," Zoey whispered.

Riley blinked at her. "You are too nice."

Zoey laughed. "No, I just try to understand people."

Riley shrugged, embarrassed. "Well... thanks for giving me a second chance."

Zoey bumped her shoulder lightly. "Friends do that."

Emma smiled quietly at the exchange.

Harper curled against the arm of the couch. "I am glad you two are okay again."

Riley nodded. "Me too."

Coach tapped her mug against her knee. "Storms reveal things." She looked at each girl. "Some weaknesses, yes. But also strength, and heart."

Zoey sank deeper under her blanket. "Saddle Creek feels different now."

"Stronger," Emma said.

"More real," Harper added.

"More like home," Riley finished.

Silence fell, but it was a warm silence. The kind that made Emma feel wrapped in something gentle and steady.

After a few minutes, the girls drifted back into the barn to finish light chores. They worked slowly, quietly, and with a peaceful rhythm. Riley swept the aisle while Zoey tossed soft bedding into Daisy's stall. Harper carried warm water buckets to Fern. Emma brushed Knightfall with long, comforting strokes, letting the repetitive motion ease the last of her tension.

The sun rose higher, brightening the barn. Dust motes danced in the golden beams. Every sound felt softer after the storm.

At one point, Riley passed Zoey a broom. Zoey thanked her. Riley smiled. It was so natural that Emma almost forgot they had spent weeks ignoring each other.

Harper hummed under her breath while filling Fern's hay net.

Emma felt a sense of peace settle deep inside her. She brushed Knightfall's mane slowly, letting the rhythm soothe them both.

"You are my brave boy," she whispered. "Thank you for trusting me."

Knightfall turned his head and nudged her shoulder, gentle and warm.

Hours passed without rush.

Coach walked by occasionally, checking on the horses and on the girls. She did not speak often. She did not need to. The mood of the barn said everything.

Late in the morning, as they gathered in the aisle to rest, Coach approached them with a soft smile.

"This barn is built from wood and nails," she said quietly. "But what holds it together is the people inside it. Last night reminded me of that."

Emma felt a lump rise in her throat.

Zoey leaned her head against Daisy's door. "I will remember that storm forever."

Harper nodded, hugging her arms around herself. "I will remember how you all helped Fern."

Riley crossed one boot over the other, glancing between the group. "I will remember how we pulled together."

Emma breathed in the warm barn air. "Me too."

Coach stepped back and studied them like a group of horses she had trained over years. "You are growing. Not just as riders. As people. That matters more than you know."

Emma felt her chest swell with something tender and strong.

Zoey whispered, "I feel like we came out of that night as different riders."

Riley nodded. "Better ones."

Harper smiled softly. "Closer ones."

Emma looked around at their faces, lit by the soft glow of the morning sun. She remembered the fear of the night. The crack of the tarp. Knightfall rearing. Fern fighting for breath. The cold. The darkness. The storm.

But she also remembered their voices steadying the horses. Their hands working together. Their hearts holding firm.

She remembered friendship repairing itself in the middle of the chaos.

She remembered bravery blooming in unexpected places.

And now, in the calm after the storm, she felt something she had not felt in a long time.

Hope.

Warm and deep and certain.

Saddle Creek was still standing.

So were they.

And together, they were stronger than any storm.

Chapter Twelve

Morning settled over Saddle Creek in soft layers of pale light, each one warmer than the last. The storm had ended fully now, leaving a stillness so complete it felt like the world was holding its breath. The sky stretched clear and pale blue. The sun glinted off snow crystals like scattered diamonds.

Emma stepped out of the barn and paused at the sight of the paddock. The fences wore thick coats of white. The trees bowed gently, their branches heavy with frost. A thin ribbon of steam lifted from the warm creek that cut through the lower pasture. Everything shimmered.

"It looks enchanted," Zoey whispered behind her.

Emma turned and smiled. "Like a fairytale."

Harper joined them, bundled in her thick coat. Her eyes still held signs of exhaustion but also brightness. "Fern ate her whole breakfast," she said proudly. "She even nibbled her hay without needing encouragement."

Emma felt warmth spread through her chest. "That is amazing."

Riley trotted up, her cheeks flushed from carrying a water bucket.

"Ruby is practically vibrating with energy. She wants out so badly she might dig a tunnel under the barn."

Zoey laughed. "We should let them out soon. They deserve something good after last night."

Coach joined them, stepping outside with her coffee cup. Her breath rose in a small cloud. "I was waiting for you to say that," she said. "The storm has passed. The air is calm. The footing looks safe in the lower field. I think the horses earned a play break."

"And a ride?" Emma asked, unable to hide the hope in her voice.

Coach smiled. "A short one. Slow pace. A walk only. The trail behind the creek will be beautiful this morning."

Zoey clapped her hands. Riley did a small fist pump. Harper bounced on her boots.

Emma could not stop grinning. "Let us tack up then."

They ran back inside, moving with more energy than they had felt in days. The barn buzzed with quiet excitement. The horses sensed it too. Knightfall perked up the moment Emma entered his stall.

"Ready for a winter ride?" she asked.

He bobbed his head, as if saying absolutely.

Emma brushed him carefully, smoothing his thick winter coat, checking each hoof to make sure no snow or ice had packed under it. She draped his saddle pad over his back, loving the comforting routine of each step. Something inside her felt restored, as if the storm had stripped away doubt and left something stronger.

Zoey hummed while saddling Daisy. Riley muttered in concentrated irritation as Ruby kept nudging her for treats. Harper took her time with Fern, though Coach walked over to help lift the saddle since the mare was still recovering.

Soon they all stood in the center aisle with their horses, ready to go.

Coach inspected each one. "Everything looks good. Stay together. If anything feels off, we stop immediately."

"Yes, Coach," the girls said in near perfect unison.

They walked outside into the bright, cold air. Snow crunched under their boots. The paddock gate groaned as Coach pushed it open. The horses stepped into the whiteness with wide eyes and cautious steps at first, then more confidence.

Knightfall lifted his tail, delighted by the soft snow. Ruby tossed her head, snorting at the cold. Daisy stretched her neck, breathing deeply. Fern walked gently, her steps slow but steady.

The world looked new, as if the storm had painted everything from scratch.

They mounted up, breath pluming into the crisp air. The saddles creaked softly. Knightfall shifted under Emma with a contented sigh.

"This is the best morning ever," Zoey said.

"It feels like the whole valley is sparkling," Harper added.

Riley tilted her face toward the sun. "And quiet. Like the world is finally resting."

Coach walked beside them for the first stretch, then nodded. "You know this trail well. Walk only. Keep space between each horse. I will follow behind."

Emma took the lead with Knightfall, who stepped forward eagerly but politely. Snow muffled every hoofbeat, making the ride feel dreamlike. The trail bent behind the barn and dipped gently toward the creek. Sunlight scattered through the trees, illuminating the path like a golden ribbon.

Zoey rode behind Emma, Daisy moving in soft, steady strides. Harper followed, Fern's hooves careful but sure. Riley and Ruby brought up the rear, the mare full of winter pride but listening well.

The trail opened into a narrow clearing where the creek shimmered under a thin skin of ice along its edges. Steam rose in delicate curls, catching sunlight in pale rainbows.

Zoey gasped. "It is like a painting."

Emma felt her throat tighten with the beauty of it. "I love this place," she whispered.

Knightfall flicked an ear back at her, sensing her emotion.

Harper leaned to pat Fern's neck. "I think Fern loves it too."

The horses walked in a line along the creek bank, breath rising in thick clouds. Snow fell gently from the branches above when a bird hopped from limb to limb.

Riley called softly from the back, "I could live in a morning like this."

Zoey smiled. "Same."

Emma led them up a small rise where the trail widened and overlooked the lower valley. From here, Saddle Creek looked peaceful and strong, the barns like warm beacons against the white landscape.

Harper sighed. "We made it through the storm."

Riley's voice softened. "Together."

Zoey glanced across the line of horses. "I am glad we talked. I missed this."

Riley nodded, cheeks pink. "Me too. For real this time."

Emma felt quiet joy fill her chest. There was nothing dramatic about this moment. No fear. No rushing. Just girls, horses, sunlight, and snow.

A winter wonderland in every sense.

They continued to the end of the ridge, where the trail turned into a loop around a small stand of evergreens. Snow shook loose as they passed under the branches, dusting their helmets and their horses' manes. Knightfall snorted playfully when flakes landed on his nose.

Emma laughed out loud.

The other girls laughed too, the sound rising into the clear air like music.

On the far side of the loop, the trail dipped between two trees and revealed a cluster of deer standing in the sunlight. The deer looked up briefly, ears turning, then lifted their tails and bounded away across the deep snow, leaving perfect tracks behind.

Harper whispered, "This is magical."

Emma agreed silently.

After a while they reached the halfway point and paused to let the horses rest. The sky brightened into a pale winter blue. A single hawk circled overhead, wings shining.

Coach caught up to them, footsteps crunching loudly in the fresh trail. She looked proud of both riders and horses.

"Everyone doing alright?" Coach asked.

"I feel perfect," Zoey said.

"Ruby wants to run," Riley replied, "but she is pretending to be polite."

Harper smiled. "Fern is good."

Emma patted Knightfall. "He could walk forever."

Coach looked toward the creek. "The valley needed a storm like that. Clears the air, strengthens the roots. Everything will grow better in spring."

Emma nodded. "So will we."

Coach saw the look between Zoey and Riley, and the peaceful strength in Harper's posture. "You girls are stronger today than you were yesterday. Storms are hard, but they teach you. And you listened."

They started the return journey, following the same trail back along the creek. The horses walked with soft satisfaction, their bodies relaxed. Emma felt the rhythm of Knightfall's steps echo inside her chest.

The sun climbed slowly behind the ridge, warming patches of the snow. Droplets fell from the branches overhead, landing like tiny cold kisses on their jackets.

As they neared the barn again, Emma felt the weight of the storm's memory settle into something softer. Something she would carry with her. A reminder of courage. A reminder of friendship.

Harper rode up beside her. "Thank you again. For helping Fern."

Emma smiled. "You helped her. We just supported you."

Harper shook her head gently. "I do not think I could have stayed calm without you."

Emma reached over and squeezed Harper's gloved hand. "We

were all scared. But that is what makes nights like that matter. We found strength in each other."

Harper's eyes shimmered. "Yes."

Behind them, Riley and Zoey chatted quietly, laughing about an icicle that had fallen onto Riley's boot earlier. They sounded like themselves again. Like a team.

Emma breathed the cold air deeply.

Saddle Creek felt like a place that held memories. The storm. The fear. The teamwork. The relief. The miracle of Fern's recovery. And this peaceful morning ride that sealed everything back together.

When they reached the barn yard again, Coach lined them up in front of her.

"You rode beautifully," she said. "Your horses trust you more after last night. And after this morning."

Zoey lifted her chin proudly. "I feel like Daisy is listening better than ever."

"She is," Coach said. "You both are."

Harper stroked Fern's neck. "She is a little tired, but she is happy."

"She is healing," Coach agreed. "Let her rest well today."

Riley patted Ruby's shoulder. "She wants to brag about surviving the storm."

Coach laughed. "Ruby brags about everything she does. That is her nature."

Emma leaned against Knightfall's neck. "Thank you for letting us ride today, Coach."

Coach nodded. "You needed it."

They dismounted slowly, savoring the last moments of the morning light. The horses shook out their manes and breathed deeply, as if stretching after a long night of tension.

Inside the barn, the warmth wrapped around them like a blanket. Saddles came off. Bridles were hung. Hooves were picked. Coats were brushed. The quiet routines felt perfect after the past twenty four hours.

Emma whispered to Knightfall, "Thank you for being brave."

He nudged her heart area, pressing soft and warm. Emma smiled deeply.

She knew this morning would stay with her forever.

Before the storm.

Through the storm.

After the storm.

They had been tested.

They had grown.

They had repaired what had been broken.

And now they were stronger than they ever imagined.

Outside, snow still glittered across the valley.

Inside, warmth and peace filled Saddle Creek.

Book Four ended not with a storm, but with sunlight.

And with it, a quiet promise that new challenges waited beyond winter.

From Saddle Creek to You

Dear rider,

Storms look frightening when they gather. They rumble. They shake the things you love. They make your heart beat faster. But storms always pass. And when they do, the world looks new again.

The Saddle Creek Riders learned that this winter. They discovered bravery they did not know they had. They repaired friendships that had started to crack. They kept each other safe when the lights went out and the wind roared. And in the end, they stepped into the sunshine stronger than before. But every season brings something new. There are rumors of a spring clinic. A visiting trainer with a reputation for changing the way riders see themselves. A new challenge that will test confidence and courage in a different way. And somewhere in the valley, a wandering ranch horse has left tracks in the snow, waiting for another season to bring him over the ridge. Storms shape us but spring grows us. See you in Book Five.

Keep riding with heart,

Wren Willowbrook

www.ingramcontent.com/pod-product-compliance
Lightning Source LLC
Chambersburg PA
CBHW071839190726
48292CB00005B/1835